I0822908

AZUL

First Printing, 2023

Dedications:

There's a lot of people who deserve thanks for this book. If you aren't mentioned here, just know that I truly appreciate your help and all you've done to help me grow as a writer/person. From every teacher I've had, to everyone who has read my work, I truly appreciate you.

I want to thank Allah for every blessing He has provided me and everything He has given me.

I want to thank my amazing family for their support (my dad, Khaled; my mom, Njela; my brothers Ahmed, Badr, and Adam; my wife, Rabia).

I want to thank my friends who've taken time out of their busy lives to hear about this book and be my test readers.

I want to thank Christy Cohen, Chersti Nieveen, and Parisa Zolfaghari for all the help they did editing and reading over this book and answering the million questions I asked them.

I want to thank you, every single one of you who bought this book (or got it as a gift). I can't express with words how much I appreciate you. You're truly the GOAT!

CONTENTS

AZUL

OMAR SOUSSI

Omar Soussi

Prologue

In the South of France

I woke up in the middle of the night to the cry of something outside. I couldn't tell what animal it was, but I knew for sure it wasn't one of ours. I lay in my bed for a minute, believing it was simply my imagination, but the constant screams erased that belief. I quietly got up from my bed and went outside, trying my hardest to avoid making any noises that would wake my father, Adam, up. As I got out, my eyes slowly adjusted to the blackness surrounding me. I could see none of our animals were awake. I noticed that it was growing louder as I walked closer to the forest surrounding our house. I was a bit concerned walking into these forests this late, but I doubted there was anyone there to take me.

I walked closer to the cries to find a small gray hound in a ditch, trying desperately to crawl out. It probably got lost from its mother and fell in one of my deer traps. The hole wasn't too deep, but large enough to keep the dog trapped.

"You okay, little baby?" I said to the adorable little beast as I reached down to grab her. At first, she growled at me, fearing that I might hurt her even more. "Don't worry, I'm not here to hurt you," I said as I grabbed her. The pup's cries went away as I held her. As she licked my face, wagging her tail, I had the urge to keep her for myself, but no doubt her family would miss her. I put the dog down, and she immediately ran north like a bolt of lightning. I walked through the forest, trying to keep up with her, and after a bit of time, we eventually found her mother and the other pups, all asleep. She joined her family, the sight of them warming my heart so much that the frigid weather surrounding me felt like a warm summer breeze.

As I turned away to walk home, another cry—one that haunted our existence—let loose through the forest. The Dragon. It was closer than usual, but not close enough that I feared for me and my father's life. The dog and her pups all woke up from the cry, each of them barking up a storm and following the mother as she sprinted to find safety. Even the pup I found left without missing a step.

The roar was over quickly, but fear still ran down my spine when I heard it. It's something no one gets over, no matter how often one hears it—and we did not hear it often, luckily. My father told me whenever he heard the Dragon, his heart skipped a beat. Our *fearless* warchief, Louis, said that he saw the Monster with his own eyes, and he couldn't shake the feeling of dread and death whenever he thought about it. I'd never seen it, but from what I knew, nothing good could come from it. That Monster destroyed the world and killed countless people. I knew some of my neighbors thought the beast looked majestic; it made me happy that I didn't spend time with them. How could something so monstrous and evil be majestic?

As I walked back to my home, I looked up at the night sky and saw it was filled with stars and the glowing moon. I gazed out, dumbfounded by its beauty, when I heard the roar once again. The sound from the Dragon was closer and was more of a lion's yell than a dog's whimper. After a few seconds, I saw out in the far distance the beast in the sky, and in that moment, all the fear in my heart rose.

I could barely make it out, but I could see its long black wings, its claws that should be coated in blood, and the crystal blue eyes everyone spoke of, though not clearly. That was the first time I saw the winged demon, and for those five seconds, I realized how insignificant I was. In a time of Dragons, what could a peasant girl do in this world?

CHAPTER 1

I woke up the next day to the usual clucks and neighs the chickens and horses make in the morning. It took me a while to fall back into a peaceful slumber after I saw the Dragon. My lungs were short of air, my head felt lighter than the clouds above, and my heart ran like a wild horse in the plains. It was the first time I'd seen the black beast, and even then, I only caught a glimpse of it, like a black shadow cutting through the sky. But the roar, that ear-shattering, earth-trembling, heart-sinking call of death. For something that I've heard for the twenty years I've been alive, it still took the air out of my lungs and squeezed the life out of my heart.

It took a second for me to hear my father's voice as he spoke with the animals outside. He had done this for the last few years, trying to find a bit of company during the times I'd hunt or go to town. What type of company those animals could provide his old yet gentle mind was for him only. It was only after I heard him ask where I was that I got out of my tiny bed. I put my itchy fur cloak over my brown gown, put my black boots on, and I started to walk out of my room to help him take care of the animals in our backyard.

We didn't have that much of a field for our animals, but it wasn't like we had that many to begin with. Three chickens, a cow, and two horses made up the "farm" we had, but we managed through it. He turned around as he heard me come outside, his expression one of wonder, yet filled with love. His body was out of shape, and his back was crooked from all the years of pain he endured, yet he wouldn't rest. His feet and his hands were filled with cuts, calluses, and wounds, but that was not enough to stop him from enjoying life, if you could call *this* life. He didn't possess my golden skin nor my crystal blue eyes and black hair, but I guess I took more from my mother's side. Most of the color on his face was the red in his cheeks and nose, the rest was a sickly, pale tone, yet he was as vibrant as anyone I knew. I saw in his left hand was his wooden cane, and in his right hand was his misbaha. The rosary beads were worn down to the point that their black paint was chipped away until it was just fine wood. He was wearing one of his two black thobes that he owned before I was born, each filled with holes and worn out to the point they were almost gray. His hazel-brown eyes had a hint of white clouds as they looked tired and bloodshot, seeing anything beyond a few feet was a minor miracle. Yet his face flipped from tired to as joyful as a child when he heard my footsteps. The last few years had been tough on us as his sight and strength slowly left, but no matter what, he always had a smile on his face.

"Azul, there you are. Thought you might've been in the forest shooting that bow around," he said in a carefree voice.

Since we had such few animals, when I was young, my father and I would go deep into the forest and either fish or hunt for food. We'd seen all manner of creatures there, like deers, wild boars, and the occasional wolf. As he got weaker, I would go by myself and hunt, finding a rabbit or a deer if we were lucky. At first, I was petrified of the forest, consumed by the idea that these wild beasts would steal me away and kill me. I even thought that the Dragon lived in that black forest and would roast us alive. But my father, he taught me how to be brave and helped me surpass my fear. He taught me how to hunt, how to survive in the wilderness, and, more importantly, how to live. I cherished those moments I spent with him, the fun we had, the lessons he taught me in that forest. My eyes begin to water up at the thought of them.

"I decided not to hunt this morning. I barely slept after I saw the Dragon," I said, my voice shifting to an uneasy feeling. His face changed from a cheerful glow to a stare of fear and confusion.

"You *saw* it?" he said with grave concern in his voice, covering his mouth with his hand like he'd seen a gruesome murder.

"The beast flew across the sky at night, after probably eating some cow or horse. It looked just as I thought it would." I stared into the sky like it was still in front of me.

"*Or* it ate a human," my father said as he recited a quick verse from the Quran and quickly bowed to Allah. My father was a religious man, devoted to a fault. He told me that before he came to this town, he worked at one of the mosques in the southern part of Spain, in a region called Granada. He spent his time helping everyone, from peasants to even the royal family in the area, all in the name of his lord Allah and his faith. He told me that he left Spain long before the Dragon ever arrived, as he heard rumors that the Spanish crown was planning on placing restrictions on Muslims in the region. So he left, leaving everyone he knew behind, and started a new life here. He never liked talking about his life in Spain, other than mentioning it was where he found my mother. Perhaps something tragic occurred there that scarred him.

When that demon broke loose on the world and plunged us into Hell, many clung to their faith as a way of protection. When word spread that the Pope and the Vatican were burned by the beast, their faith slowly died with their leaders. Why believe in a God when He allowed his Holy City to burn, when he abandoned his followers and allowed this monster to roam the world? Yet in a world where loyalty can be forgotten in an instance, my father never gave up his faith in Allah.

"Could've been a person, but I doubt it," I said, shrugging my shoulders. While my dad was loyal to Allah, my faith was like glass hitting the floor, fractured. There were parts of the religion I cared for, but I never felt a connection to it. I could never tell him that, for I feared it would shatter his fragile heart, yet I felt like he knew. When I was growing up, he taught me about Islam, though he never demanded that I follow it. I just couldn't attach myself to any God, not when the devil roamed the earth freely and Allah did nothing to stop it. According to my father, Allah knew what we could handle and that He was the All-Merciful, but how could I believe that when the Dragon existed? How could I pray to Him or any savior when They've forsaken us? The only person I could believe in was myself.

"Well, as long as we have Allah watching over us, we'll be fine. Can't do anything toward that beast, so we may as well focus on what we need to do here at home and help those in need," he said with hope and sincerity in his voice. It's impressive just how much faith he still had, with everything that had happened to us.

"You're right, Father, can't be worried about things out of our control," I said to him with a pinch of happiness in my voice and a smile on my face as I hugged and kissed his bald head, practically towering over him.

This mindset wasn't just ours; everyone left in this hellhole knew if that fiend came near you, you were dead. There were men who believed they were chosen by God to slay the beast, yet they all failed. The land we live in was once known as France, and our last "king," Francis the Foolish as we call him, was one of those men. Rumors spread that he had a dream as a child that fire surrounded him and that he used a sword to wipe it all away in one swing. When he heard that a fire-breathing beast destroyed the land west of us known as Spain, he believed that dream was a prophetic tale to him by God. He rallied the French army, and within a week, thirty-five thousand men marched from Paris to hunt down the Dragon. He proclaimed himself the savior of France, Europe, and Catholicism, as he swore his army would kill the beast. Personally, I believed the man saw an opportunity to claim control over Europe. With Spain gone, no one in Europe would dare oppose his rule, especially if he succeeded in killing the Dragon. I don't believe in prophetic dreams, but I do believe in an opportunistic man taking advantage of the gullibility of the dumb and blind.

But there was no prophetic slaying of the beast, nor did God come down and save those who believed in Him. The Dragon laid waste to Francis and his army within a week after they rode, and France collapsed immediately after. Paris was purged by the peasants demanding food. The royal palace, along with the family, was torched during the purge. Even though the Dragon didn't destroy France the way it did Spain, the people fought over land and power, and eventually, France was nothing but a bunch of small cities that would trade with each other and no more.

This was the reality that the world faced with the rise of the Dragon. If the flames didn't kill you, the disease and lack of supplies did. Kingdoms would fall under this instability, kings and lords were murdered by their peasants, rebellions sparked across the land, and millions of men, women, and children were killed because of it, staining the earth with their blood.

The world fell into a new Dark Age with no end in sight. Rumors spread that England burned their ships and refused to allow anyone from mainland Europe, cutting themselves off and fending for themselves. Spain was completely obliterated by the Dragon and barely anyone survived there. The Holy Roman Empire and Germanic city-states were burnt to the ground, and that's all we've heard from our *fearless* lord Louis. The Christian faith was all but extinct after the Pope died. There weren't any other Muslims I knew besides my father or any other followers of Judaism, but I assumed the same could be said for them. Many gave up on their religion or would find something else to pray toward. Some went back to the pagan gods their ancestors worshipped, like the Moon or Sun, some went to worshipping their warlords as gods, and some worshipped the Dragon itself, saying it arrived to burn away the sins of the world. I knew a man in the village who was convinced that the Dragon was Jesus reincarnated, returning to punish the nonbelievers. It's people like him that make me so happy I stay at home and rarely spend time in the village with those idiots. Some men, like Louis, would attack someone who believed in Jesus or any God besides himself. He viewed his might as the great equalizer and his voice as the only Holy Word we would need to follow.

That Dragon changed everything, and no moment has passed where we didn't think we could be the next region to perish. My village, Toulouse, was small but was right next to the Desert of Bones, what we call the country formerly known as Spain. Rumors spread rapidly throughout the village that the Dragon lived there, though no one had proven it was true or even wanted to. If it was true, it would probably take about a few minutes for it to come and destroy us. The hair on my spine and arms stood up for a second just from that thought alone. After I fed the animals and gathered their milk and eggs, I started to walk my father back inside when he reminded me that today was Tax Day, as if I could forget.

"Don't worry, Father, we have enough to satisfy Louis," I replied to him as I placed him back in his tiny bed so he could relax. I went to the bag that sat next to his bed to see how much we had. Twelve tiny pieces of silver, two pieces of bronze, and my father's worn-out Quran that Louis would certainly not appreciate. My dad told me when he came here, he had two pieces of gold, a hundred silver pieces, and fifty bronze pieces. We've been coasting off that for years, but now, our *frivolous* spending was catching up to us. I took a quarter of the silver, headed out to the front of our house, and waited for my lord to arrive. It took some time, but I eventually heard the hooves of his men's horses come from the forest. Twenty years ago, before I was born and the arrival of the black beast, my father came here and found this house abandoned by its former owner, leaving us separated from the rest of the village. If you walked from the center of the town to here, it would take about twenty minutes, but there weren't a lot of people in our town who'd visit us.

Alas, Louis the *Bold* finally arrived in front of our home with what looked like ten men behind him. Right off the bat, his newly minted chain-link armor grabbed my attention, as did the sword on his side. You'd think you wouldn't be able to afford new weapons and armor if you owned a village with less than a hundred "grueling peasants," as he put it. But I guess when you controlled the blacksmith, you got whatever you wanted for free. Before the beast, we would be under the King's control, there would be a lord and knight who controlled the land and people, but the King was in charge. I believe it was called Feudalism, but much like the last kings, it's a dead concept. Now, it's the strongest who ran the shots, and unfortunately, Louis was our lord. We were only slightly better than slaves. Sure, we had some freedoms, but his word was law, and his orders were like the words of God.

Over his armor, I could see his disgustingly long black beard that reached his stomach and his beer belly, which practically popped out of the armor. He removed his helmet and waved around his nasty hair, giving it a chance to breathe as it was covered in sweat and grease. He smelled like he was sleeping with the pigs, which was his usual scent. Every time he came, his hair looked like it was trying to escape him, receding like the moons passing us. Though he looked like he did last month, I noticed he had a new scar on his left eye, which told me someone tried to test their luck against this forty-year-old bastard, probably one of his own men. Whoever it was, I presumed their head was on a spike at his home.

"How are you doing, gorgeous?" Louis said to me from firmly atop his horse, with a wink and a sick, deluded smile on his face. His teeth were rotten to the core, yellow, and some were unsurprisingly missing. I wanted to vomit from the sight of him and his disgusting attempt at flirting. It's times like that where I wished I was burnt alive by the Dragon.

"I'm fine, Louis, how about you?" I said with the best attempt at a pleasant tone and smile. I could feel myself dying on the inside, but I wasn't going to put us at risk so I could pout.

"Better now that I get to see you, my *belleza*," he said as he shot a kiss at me. Oh good, he tried his Spanish on me. I didn't know that a single word—beauty—could make me want to vomit, but I swallowed my pride and continued to smile. Though we live close to the remains of Spain, my father and I were the only two Spanish folks here. Most of the villagers didn't care that we were Spanish since nationality died with the old kingdoms. Louis, however, brought it up whenever he could. Maybe it was his attempt to remind me that I was different; maybe it was his attempt to embarrass me. I took a deep breath through my nose and walked up to the human ogre, never once moving my eyes away from him. Though I feared for our lives, a part of me refused to allow this bastard to intimidate me.

"Here's our tax. Hope you're satisfied," I said as I placed the pieces of silver out for him to grab. He got off his horse and got right in my face, his breath nearly knocking me over, but I refused to back down. Call it stubbornness or a death wish, but I didn't move. He ripped the coins out of my hands and took a bite of them to make sure they were "true silver." Once he finished counting, he again gave me that disgusting smirk, pumping his chest up and towering over me. I was five foot six, and he had a full foot on me at least.

"I'm always satisfied protecting the people of Toulouse. Maybe the next time I come, we can spend some quality time," Louis said to the laughter of the men behind him. My fist was so tight, I felt I could crush an apple in it. The only thought in my mind was all of the ways I could kill him. Then I realized he'd probably kill me before I got the chance.

"Unlikely," I said, grinding my teeth to each other. For the last year, he'd tried this garbage on me. The repulsive fact was I think he enjoyed seeing me squirm and resist more than the thought of actually sleeping with me. All he'd need to do is threaten to kill my father, and he'd have his way with me, but he had never done that. I took a step back to get some space, only for Louis to match it. He put one of his hands on my hair, and it took every fiber of my being to not throw a punch.

"A shame. You're easily the most beautiful woman I've ever met. Your gorgeous, golden skin; your beautiful, perfect face; the way your nose and chin are just small enough to be cute but unique enough to have their own beauty. Your breasts have my heart racing, the way you make that peasant gown look so damn sexy, your luscious black hair, and those eyes. Those blue eyes look like two crystals shining off the light of the moon." His eyes scanned me as if I were stripped of my clothes.

The way he described my face and body brought back the taste of my dinner from last night and drained all my energy. I wasn't sure why he lusted for me so much, though I dreaded the thought of trying to understand this bastard's mind. It was a sick joke to him, a way he could humiliate me for my refusal to sleep with him. Perhaps he viewed the other women in our town as ugly, though I hardly doubted he was the type to only have sex with one or two women. Just the thought of the rumors I had heard about Louis made the tiny hairs on my spine rise.

The only thing I knew was I hated everything about him, especially how he greatly exaggerated my looks.

I knew I was pretty, but I certainly wasn't the most gorgeous girl in the world, and I wasn't trying or wanting to be. My hair was a mess; I never fixed it, always leaving it in a bun since it usually got dirty when I hunted. My face was covered with acne and small cuts. My nose and chin were tiny, sure, and maybe they carried a unique trait, but whenever I saw them, they were small and slightly awkward. My teeth were hardly perfect, but they weren't rotten like this donkey's. My hands weren't exactly ladylike, nor was my body. If anything, they were more manly since I worked the field and hunted. I had more muscular definition than most of the women in the village but that probably had to do with me being quite skinny. My breasts weren't massive, nor were they tiny; they were of average size. My looks wouldn't save me and my father; my skills would. Sure, if the demon didn't roam the world, maybe marriage could've saved my family, but that wasn't the world we lived in today. All Louis did with his description of me was make me want to bury my head in the dirt and hide every time he'd come over. However, I knew my father wouldn't be able to deal with Louis in the condition he was in. He'd probably mention Muhammad or Allah and get himself murdered.

"I'd *kill* to have you with me," he whispered as he leaned closer to my face. I tried to back off, but his hand was right on my hip, holding me still. I kept myself from shuddering, but only just as I felt his breath on my cheek. I didn't want to look or give him any idea that I was miserable, but I didn't think I had the skills to fake it. "But if I'm being honest, seeing you squirm whenever I come by, *that* gives me so much joy." I pushed him aside then, not too harshly—he was already backing off—but enough that he and his men laughed their asses off from it. "Till next time, Azul." He leaped back onto his horse and rode off with his men, who started howling like mad dogs. What a bunch of pigs, especially Louis. They're a bunch of pigs that just so happened to control our lives.

I went back to my house and worked on my daily chores. It was a small place, mostly made up of two rooms my father made and a tiny kitchen. We had a little fireplace in the kitchen where we cooked and huddled in front of during the frigid winter nights. Since I did most of my work yesterday, there wasn't that much left for me. I washed our clothes and hung them last night. The home was as clean as possible, so I chopped some wood and set up a small fire. All I needed to do was get dinner ready for me and my father. I didn't mind doing all this work. When I was younger, my father did all this by himself. It was the least I could do for him in his old age and condition.

I went to the kitchen to start preparing for dinner. A small potato, two tomatoes, and a quarter head of lettuce, all stale. Guess we'd have some form of a stew tonight. I cut the vegetables up, took the remainder of the chicken we had from last night, and placed it in our small iron bowl. Poured some water, some salt, and *voila*, our dinner for tonight. I placed the pot on top of the low flames to begin cooking. It would take a couple hours for everything to mix together, plenty of time for me to stock up on food. I went back to my father's room to see he was in his chair right next to the window, appreciating the calming sounds that nature was providing him. The weather was perfect; there was a light breeze that buried the heat. It must be like heaven to him.

"I'm heading to get us some more food," I whispered to him while crouching down to give him a quick kiss on his head. He lightly grasped my hand and gave it a quick kiss, then whispered back to me, "Enjoy yourself, my child."

I rarely spent time in the village; even when I was younger, we wouldn't go there often. We wanted nothing to do with Louis, and since he spent most of his time there, drinking and having his *fun*, it made a lot of sense to stay away. The village was small, not much larger than what I imagined a usual farming town in Europe would be before the Dragon. With everything that's transpired here, I'd imagine we might've grown a bit if it wasn't for his terrible rule. For as long as I can remember, Louis has ruled, and we've endured it. We make just enough food to sustain ourselves, and due to the trading we make with each other, we're able to *just* pay our taxes, though some of us pay with our food or *favors*. After the fall of France and the world, our money has basically been whatever valuable resource we own. For some, it's silver and bronze; for others, it's plants and animals; for the rare few, it's their trades and skills.

As I got closer to the town, I could see Louis's tower stalking over the people. The tower was about three floors tall, but that third floor was renovated to a makeshift watchtower. From what my father told me, the tower was made about fifty years ago when Spain was attempting to push into France. It served as a watchtower to warn of incoming invasions. However, the soldiers weren't able to cut down the thick forest surrounding us to make it worthwhile, which led to them abandoning the project. When Louis arrived, he must've decided to have it finished as a monument of his greatness. Even with how high it was, I could never see it from my house.

As I entered the town, I could feel my energy seemingly sapped away as the look on the people's faces screamed depression. The village was mostly made up of homes that had farms and ranches next to them. There was no wall, nothing separating us from nature, separating us from ourselves. Usually, people traded outside of their homes, but we did have enough space in the center just in case. Besides the tower and the blacksmith's place, most of these houses looked the same. Obviously, I wasn't the only one Louis tormented today. I tied my horse and went about my usual routine. I met with the redhead farmer, Bella, and bought some eggs and two baguettes from her husband, Victor, who baked and fished. I knew they just had a child since Bella's stomach had shrunk slightly from last week and I could hear the baby wailing in their home as she ran to her. After that, I went and visited the town's elder, Pierre, one of my favorite people in the world. I've known the man since I was born; he was just as old as my father, and he has been nothing less than an angel to us. As I walked to his house, I could pick up a conversation he was having with some of the children who wanted to know about the world before the Dragon. The topic brought back some of my old memories as I used to harass him, begging to know more about this world before the demon rose from the West. Based on what he was saying, it appeared he was giving them the same answer he gave me all those years ago.

"The only difference between now and the past is instead of a king we're sending our food and loyalty to, we're sending it to Lord Louis. We still fight with each other, we still pray to the gods, we still scratch and claw to survive," he said with a small smile as he stroked his white beard with his thin, dark fingers. I knew there was more to what he said, but it wasn't like there was a history book to check against or someone else we could talk to who would prove him wrong. My father would basically back whatever Pierre said and has told me numerous times that Pierre knows so much more than he does. Most of the town was younger than him, so they relied on his knowledge to survive.

Much like my father, Pierre had lost most of the hair on his head, but his beard was quite long, past his neck. He was thin, probably due to being malnourished, but few of us here weren't. His skin was wrinkly and cracked from how dry it was, looking like dark brown, almost black, leather. However, he had a sense of happiness that glowed through him. His smile could light up a room, and his voice always had a ring of content to it, like nothing could bring him down.

The same couldn't be said for the children as their faces screamed disappointment—they refused to believe what he said. For those kids, the world before the beast seemed like a fairytale, a place where knights and kings ruled and brave men traveled the seas for untold riches. It was a cruel twist for them, to hear the world barely changed, a fact they had no way to disprove. As I grew up, I would spend much of my time with Pierre since he was one of the few people who came to my house. I noticed he didn't have his walking stick, perhaps his back and knees felt strong today. I also noticed he stuck with his bold fashion statement of worn-out black pants, worn-out black flip-flops, and a worn-out white shirt. As the kids started to disperse from him, I walked up to the old man.

"I see you're still crushing children's curiosity," I said with a chuckle. He also laughed at the joke, and his smile felt like I was reuniting with a long-lost friend.

"Ah, they'll come back, just like you. The thing with curiosity is you can't crush something when there's no limit to it, and if they're anything like you, I might be hearing these questions even after I die," Pierre said, and I giggled in response. "Oh, I see that my suffering is funny. Glad to know that, Azul. How's your father?"

"He's good. He was resting by his bed when I left and didn't meet with our *fearless* leader, Louis." I looked around just to make sure no one would have a problem with what I said.

"Quite the bold statement to make about our liege lord. I hope for your sake you were more respectful to him when you're in front of him," Pierre said with a look of concern on his face.

"I was as respectful as I could be with him," I said with a tone that hinted to my true feelings about the creep, though I avoided making eye contact with Pierre. When our eyes finally met, Pierre glared at me like how a disappointed father glared at their children. He knew I was smart enough to not anger Louis, but he also didn't appreciate my willingness to openly disrespect the man. He claimed that doing so put us at risk, but this town would rather have Satan ruling it than Louis. Or at least, that's the feeling I got. There was no love lost for him.

"Is he making any progress?" he asked with sincerity, switching the topic.

"Not that much, he can barely move without a cane, but his mind has improved a bit. He's had some nightmares where he's talking about some promise, but that's not too bad," I replied while messing with the dirt. I don't like talking about what happened to my father. It was bad enough I saw the results of it daily; I didn't like having to go through it with other people too, though Pierre is a good friend, so I understand.

It had been close to three years since my dad collapsed in the middle of town. We were walking around, looking to buy some food. His hand was constantly on his chest, but we thought it was nothing, until, suddenly, he dropped to the floor. I didn't know what to do, how to help him, how to save him. I tried to wake him up and get someone, anyone, to help us. Eventually some of the villagers helped and brought him home, but there was nothing else we could do. I sat by him, waiting for some miracle to save him. The seconds passed like days, the minutes felt like weeks, and the hours were like years. Eventually he woke up, though it affected him drastically. His body was severely weakened; he could barely walk, let alone take care of the animals. His mind was weakened too; he struggled to remember details from the past or have long conversations. He didn't die, but he was crippled. He refused to let it define him; he didn't allow this to be something that would hold him back no matter how debilitated his body was. Sometimes, in the darkest crevices of my mind, I wished he did die just so he wouldn't have to suffer and live this crippled life. It's a horrible thought, and I would usually push it out the second I thought it. Seeing him miserable killed me. How could I even think like that, let alone tell Pierre, the closest thing we had to a friend, about it? Not exactly being a *great daughter* with that thought. How could I wish that the only family I have should be dead? Yet was it truly awful to want your father to rest and not live a tormented life?

"Well, I'm glad he has a great daughter like you to help him out. God knows what would happen if he was left to his own devices," Pierre said as he patted me on my back. I looked at him; his face was calming, like he knew what I was going through, but he had no judgment on it. Perhaps he knew, perhaps he didn't and was simply being kind. Regardless, I gave him a smile back and hugged him.

"I should go back; he's probably wondering where I went off. See you soon, Pierre," I said as I walked back to my horse, waving goodbye to him.

I put the baguette and eggs in my horse's satchel and rode off to my house. As I started to ride back, I noticed a young boy sitting by himself on the outskirts of town, away from the homes and near the forest. He seemed like he was eleven, maybe twelve, but he looked worn down. His face was covered with dirt and cuts, his clothes were raggedy, he was almost as skinny as a branch. I'd never met the boy; he didn't seem like the bunch that would go to Pierre's home. He was looking down, trying to hide in the shade. Perhaps his parents died recently, perhaps they just died by Louis's hands and he was thrown out. Regardless, it felt wrong to ride away from him without helping. I got off the horse and walked to the boy, his face still looking down. I crouched to him and, with a smile on my face, placed a loaf of bread and six pieces of silver in front of him. It didn't matter that we needed the food and coin; this kid didn't have anything. At least I could hunt if we got desperate.

His face lit up slightly, as much as he possibly could. He lifted his head up, holding back tears, and presented a big yet emotional smile. He whispered weakly to me, "Thank you," tears slowly pouring down his face. I nodded silently and walked back to my horse to return home.

The ride was quick and quiet, about five minutes. I placed the remaining bread and eggs in the house and checked on the food, which hadn't started boiling yet, so I decided I would go on a hunt. I grabbed my bow and arrows and changed from my gown and cloak to a white blouse and black pants. As I headed out, I walked by my father, who was still in the same spot as I left him, inside watching the animals, or at least he stared at their vicinity.

"I'm going to go on a quick hunt, and then I'll come back to finish cooking," I said to him. He nodded his head in agreement and wished me luck as I started to take my usual path into the forest.

Our town sat very close to the Garonne River, right in the middle of the forest. Some of the people in the village felt a bit concerned about the predators that lived there, however they weren't as bad as the men we paid to "protect" us. I always went north when I entered the forest, further away from the town. That way I was less inclined to run into other people. For the most part, if any traders or soldiers came to our village, they came from the south side. Though some would be concerned to walk these forests by themselves, it felt like a second home for me. In all my time going through here, whether by myself or with my father, I'd never seen another human.

A soft sound of dried leaves crunching caught my attention. I looked around and found the cause: a rabbit hopping around about twenty yards away from me. I silently readied my bow and arrow, lined my shot up, took one deep breath, released the bow, and *whoosh*, I got the little guy. I walked over to my prize with the confidence of a king and saw I got him right in the head. As I took out the arrow, I heard a bush rattle near me. *What was that,* I thought to myself as I loaded up my bow. It sounded too large for a rabbit. I heard a leaf crackle under something's footsteps. I tried to remain calm, trying to think about what it could be. My right knee started to twitch uncontrollably, my chest was rising and falling like a branch shaking in the wind, my stomach felt like there was a tornado pounding inside. The steps got louder and louder as each second passed. I kept looking around to find this beast. I turned around to see a young girl, no more than ten, sprinting in my direction. She was looking behind her like she was prey escaping her predator. She noticed me and screamed something in a language I didn't understand, running and cowering right behind me and pointing in the direction she came. The girl had no shoes, a ragged dress, and long black hair. Her skin was brown, similar to mine but darker, and her eyes were a vibrant purple. I saw her tiny chest jumping with fear, and it sounded like her lungs were about to give out any second. Before I could say a word, I saw what she was running from. One of Louis's men came sprinting toward us.

I held onto the girl's hand and looked down to see her face was rattled with fear. As he noticed the girl stopped running, he did too, giving me a better view of him. The bastard was about six feet tall, with leather armor covering his chunky body. He wore a leather helmet, but even with it, I could see his long walnut-colored hair and his chinstrap of a beard. As he got closer, his face was one of lust and desire. His bloodshot olive eyes stared only at the girl, but he started to glare at me like I was a piece of meat. His short arms held a wooden club and nothing else. He was about twelve feet out as I pointed my bow and arrow at him. He saw it and simply chuckled.

"What the hell do you want?" I screamed at him. I was yelling in hopes that someone could come to help but I knew it would do me no good. We were twenty minutes from my father and at least forty minutes from anyone who could *actually* do anything.

"That girl, I found her wandering out here all alone, and all I'm trying to do is help her out," he said in a demented tone, keeping his eyes on the child. His words were slurred; he clearly had some awful plans for this girl. "Though now that I mention it, maybe both of you need help," he said while licking his disgusting lips.

"We're good. You need to get out of here before you do something you'll regret," I said firmly back to him, trying to bury my doubt and fears. I knew a bit about how to fight, but not against someone who's spent their entire life fighting. Maybe he'd back off if I kept the bow trained on him.

"I'll tell you what, you leave the girl, and I'll let you walk away," the scumbag said to me, keeping his smug, drunk smile up. The girl gripped my pants even tighter after hearing that, like she knew what was at stake. A small voice emerged in my head, perhaps it was the devil whispering. *Abandon the girl, no harm would come to you, think about your father, what would happen if you die?* I shook my head in frustration. How could I even think like that? I couldn't abandon this child to this monster, not without putting up a fight.

"Run, and don't stop till you get to the first house and hide there, okay?" I whispered to the girl while keeping my eyes on the man and softly nudging her off. I could tell she left since her grip disappeared from my leg and his eyes went from her to me.

"You're going to have to kill me if you want her," I proclaimed to the soldier. The doubt was gone in my voice, left with only resolve and instincts.

"That can be arranged," he said with a sick lust in his voice. He sprinted to the right of me, trying to take my shot away. I fired and just missed his shoulder; he took a swing with his club to my head. I got out of the way just in time with a quick roll and turned around to see he was staring at me with the eyes of a wolf. He looked on edge, antsy. I bet he was completely inebriated, and that liquor gave him the courage to do this. I had to use speed to win.

I dropped my bow and grabbed the knife from my arrow satchel. The arrows would slow me down; the knife would give me something to defend myself with. I kept it there to kill any animals that weren't dead, but I would need to stand tall here if I wanted to live.

He stumbled over to me, swinging his wooden weapon with all his might. I was able to dodge the forceful blows; there was no speed behind them but plenty of power. He kept swinging at me, and I dodged until he got tired.

After the seventh swing, he was wheezing, desperate for air to enter his lungs. I took my opportunity to strike, sprinting right at him, knife in hand. I leaped right at his face; he caught my hand, but my force drove us to the ground. I pushed with all my might to force the blade into his face, but I was unable to do it. His death grip around my wrist nearly broke it, but I kept pushing. He used his other hand to punch my right cheek, and my face got a shock of pain that coursed through my body. I felt my cheek starting to swell up, most likely broken.

I tried to crawl away, but he immediately grabbed my hair and pushed my face right into the dirt, suffocating me, drowning me in darkness. I felt him driving his knee into my spine, nearly breaking it in half. The dirt started to enter my mouth as I tried to push him off, each breath forcing more dirt in than the next. My legs and arms were swinging wildly as I tried to hit him and get some distance between us. I started to pass out, I could feel my limbs go numb, but I wouldn't give in, not without exerting everything I had. I kept pushing and swinging my limbs, hoping one would hit his face; it felt like nothing worked until, suddenly, the weight on me lifted. I turned around and saw he was across the forest, at least ten feet away from me. I couldn't process what happened. I regained consciousness and spat the dirt out of my mouth and lungs. My ears were ringing, my nose felt like it was gone, my eyes were still foggy; I couldn't be closer to death than right now.

He stared at me, wild-eyed and mad with anger. He immediately sprinted at me, panting like a dog, and tackled me. He wrapped his thick, wet hands around my throat, squeezing the life right out of me. I scratched and clawed at anything I could get my hands on, whether it was his hands or his disgusting face, but nothing could get him off me. Just as I regained my feelings, I could feel them fading away. My attempts to get him off were weakening, my kicks for room were less powerful as time passed. As I started to black out, to my death, I saw him preparing to kiss me like the sick freak he was, taking my last breath and my life. With every fiber of my being, I gave him a lasting gift as I slammed my head to his face. I felt his warm, sticky blood on my body, and a tooth lodged in my forehead. I dropped to the ground as his steel grip around my throat vanished, his body dropping right next to me. I must've knocked him out, I tried to move, but my body was exhausted. I knew it wasn't safe to stay—he could wake up at any moment—but I couldn't move, my body started to shut down, and soon, I fell into a dark slumber.

CHAPTER 2

I found myself awake in the forest with the moon's light glaring over me. My body was numb. I couldn't feel anything except the cold wind cutting me down like a lumberjack chops a tree. The pain I felt before this was gone, my throat, my lungs, my chest, nothing. *Is this a dream, or did I actually die*, I wondered to myself. My mind became flooded with countless thoughts: *is anyone looking for me, did that girl find safety, would anyone find my rotted carcass, what would happen to my father?* As my body began to thaw and I could finally move, I started to walk through the forest. It didn't take long for me to discover I was wearing a turquoise dress, fueling the thought that death had taken me from this world. As I walked, my memories started to play within the shadows of the forest. I saw the nights where me and my father would go to bed hungry, but we wouldn't complain since we had each other. I saw myself go from a smile to a look of shock as he passed out, I saw a memory of me playing with a boy but his face was covered by the shadows.

More memories flashed before me. I tried to run away from it all, memories of me hunting, playing with my dad, riding my horse. One memory took my attention, though; it was a woman screaming in a pool of blood, and I saw her holding a child. I couldn't see her face, but I could tell from the eyes of that child, it was me. Was that my mother? I reached out, hoping to escape into that memory and live with her for the rest of my existence, but it disappeared right in front of me. The memory crushed my chest harder than that drunk ass did. My mother died giving birth to me, and my father never talked about her. I never knew who she was, what happened to her, or anything. I didn't even know her name. She was buried in my mind since I knew so little, locked away so I wouldn't feel that pain. I knew my father loved her so much that he couldn't even think about her without breaking down. As I looked up, two clouds were waiting in front of me, like they were waiting for me to arrive. They each took the shape of a body, but I couldn't recognize who they were. I saw from the way they held each other's hands that they had so much love and tenderness for each other.

"We're so proud of you, Azul," the one on the right said in an angelic voice.

"We love you with all our heart," the one on the left said, his voice sterner and more hardened but filled with love. My heart and mind were racing. I didn't know what was happening, who these people were, where I was. Had I died? Were these angels sent down to bring my soul into Jannah? Or was my mind playing a cruel trick on me? It all came rushing toward me, and I let it all out in one scream. "What's going on?!"

They stuck their hands out to me, and as I reached out to grab them, they burst into flames that began to spread through the forest. The flames weren't hurtful, they weren't suffocating me, nor did they burn me. I tried to break through the flames, but they were impenetrable. They were never-ending, rising higher as the seconds passed. My heart was pounding as I covered my mouth in fear, and for a second, everything went dark and the world went silent. I heard a voice call out to me, sounding like a death rattle. The voice repeated the same line to me, each time getting louder. "Remember who you are, use your gifts to protect your people, and believe." I saw two giant sapphire eyes staring at me like a predator tracking its meal and fire roaring right at me as I screamed for my life. As the flames reached my body, I finally woke up, panting and drenched in sweat.

I woke up in my bed, covered in bandages and a wet towel on my lap that was probably on my head. As I tried to sit up, a stinging sensation ran across my face and throat, reminding me of the fight I'd just survived. I slowly reached to my forehead and felt the small dent there from the tooth that was lodged in from my last act. I knew from how sore my right arm and back were that I was in a bad way. I looked at my arm and saw the wrist was practically purple from his death grip; I imagined my spine was just the same. I glanced down to my blanket and saw it was covered in blood, blood I could still taste in my mouth. Despite how much it tortured my body, I started to sit up and saw my father staring at me as if I was a demon. His face was warped by fear and concern. I couldn't tell what he thought happened to his girl, but I could tell from his blood-stained hands that he'd been taking care of me for a while.

"Are you all right? You've been asleep for a long time now," he asked me after a few seconds of silence, still keeping his distance like I might freak out or scream.

I didn't know if I could answer that; my throat felt crushed, and I could barely speak. But the fact I could breathe with only a bit of pain told me that I had survived this flirt with death.

"Well enough for me to help around the house," I said as I tried to get out of my bed, but like the strings of a puppet, my back refused to let that happen. A soft yelp had my father immediately leaping to my side, ready to help as he placed me back onto the bed, back to rest. "How long was I out?" I whispered.

"Nearly a full day," he responded, looking at me like he saw me die numerous times, his mouth covered by his hand as he clearly tried to fight off tears.

My eyes grew wide after hearing what my father said. I felt my heart skip a beat. I couldn't believe it. "A full day?" I said, fear and shock in my voice, the pain disappearing for that brief moment. I knew it had to be a while. There was no sun out, the candles surrounding us clearly showed time had passed, but an entire day? How did I survive? How did that ogre not kill me?

"What happened to that bastard?" I asked, a hint of terror in my voice, fearing that he might've kidnapped us. There's no way he would've let me live. My father looked at me with his eyebrows raised like I was trying to make a joke.

"What are you talking about? You killed him," he said with a bit of sarcasm in his voice. "His head was smashed to pieces."

The world went silent in that second. I couldn't hear the crickets chirping, the fire cracking the wood, the wind tossing around the tree branches. I couldn't believe it. My life was all but over when I head-butted him. I hoped he would bite his tongue off as my last gift to him, but how could it kill him? I buried my head in my hands as all these thoughts ran through my mind; the world felt so tiny, and everything was squeezing into me like I was a grape. My mind slowed down as an obvious thought popped up, and I lifted my head and looked at my father.

"How did you find me?" I asked with confusion in my voice. My father scratched his head. Eventually his hand found itself on his cheek.

"I was in my chair when I heard something in the bushes. I started to walk over, and when I realized there was nothing there, I heard you scream. I rushed to the town, yelling for help. The only person who offered to help me was Charles, the farm boy. He joined me to look for you, and he was the one who found you on the ground unconscious. He helped me clean your wounds and with other trivial tasks this old man can't handle," he said, laughing.

That child, was that who my father heard? It sounded like she got away safely, but where was she if not here? Maybe she made it to the town. Maybe she returned to her own home once she got us help. But where was her home? I'd never seen her in our town. I'd have to check later since it was clear she wasn't here.

That name, though. Charles. It'd been years since I heard it. He was a quiet, twenty-one-year-old man with hair black as the night and a goofy smile that would make anyone happy. We knew each very well for years, but as my father's body weakened, relationships that didn't matter faded. That name, hearing what he did, I could feel the pressure surrounding my body loosen. My mind relaxed, and the darkness surrounding me started to fade as it was replaced by a small light, like a candle in the middle of the forest.

"Did he ask for anything?" I said weakly, my hands dropping from my face to my side.

"No, but I gave him some food and some of our bronze for his help. He told me to let him know how you're doing once you're awake," he said with a smile on his face, taking my hand. Food and some bronze, not even silver. I doubted Charles demanded that after he was done helping. We hadn't talked in years. Why help someone who forgot about you?

"All right, my darling, I need you to eat and then get some more rest. I'll bring you a bowl of stew," he said as he took the now dry cloth off my forehead to re-soak it. The cold water felt refreshing on my burning head, like the rain hitting my body on a hot summer day. Though the news of Charles brought a ray of light to me, I still felt like death. The stew my father gave me was quite delicious, though I guess anything would taste like the finest fruit from the Garden of Eden when you're starving. After I devoured the bowl, he kissed my head and said to me, "Goodnight, my sweet angel," while pinching my cheek and giving me a warm smile. Right as he left the door, a thought hit me like a mountain of bricks.

"Father, who was my mother?" I asked him. His smile turned into a cold, stern stare, like all life was sucked out of his soul. He stood there for a second, thinking about what his next words would be, stroking his chin.

"Your mother..." He started to speak before he had to cover his mouth. He stood there, just thinking of the right words to say. "She was the bravest woman I'd ever met." That was a usual answer from him, something vague and non-descriptive. I knew it was still a sore spot for him, for he clearly cared for her even after all these years. It never gave me the satisfaction I wanted or needed. I wanted more this time. I *needed* more. That nightmare and my dance with death brought out this demand.

"Yes, but... who was she? I don't even know her name or anything about her," I said to him, trying to keep my composure. I could see in his eyes the pain that these questions dragged out of him. I hated how much pain this put my father through, but I couldn't go to my grave without that knowledge. I *needed* it. I deserved some information on her at the very least.

"You're right," he said as he sat next to me, taking a deep breath to gather his thoughts. "It isn't fair I hide this information from you.... Her name was Sara, she was just like you, headstrong, a bit of a troublemaker, but someone with a massive heart who was loyal to the very end," he said as he tried to keep his emotions under wraps, wiping away any tears from his eyes and taking deep breaths through his nose. "Above all else, she strived to be a good person and do right for those around her, no matter the cost."

I saw that the tears were starting to run off his cheek like a waterfall. The man lost the love of his life and nearly lost his daughter, his only family left in this hell. I should've waited until I fully recovered before I made this demand, before I acted too selfishly. I put my bowl down, slowly and painfully moved toward him, placing my hand on his shoulder.

"I'm sorry I've made you bring up these old memories. I know she meant a lot to you, and I just wanted to know her," I said softly to him. I've always felt guilty about her death. I knew she died giving birth to me, and though there was nothing I could do about it, perhaps if I never existed, she would still be alive right now. Maybe my father wouldn't have had that accident. I knew it was worthless to think like that, but that didn't mean I stopped doing so.

"Don't apologize, my sweet child. Those memories are why she's never truly gone. She's always with us right there." He pointed at my head and his heart. "Now you need your rest. Goodnight, Azul," he said as he kissed my forehead.

"Goodnight, Father," I responded as I lightly kissed his hand and gave him a warm smile before I returned to a deep slumber.

The next day I felt like I had emerged from a cocoon. My body had healed remarkably. When I took the bandages off, the wounds and bruises were gone, though they left some scars on me. The dent on my forehead was also gone, and my throat and wrist felt like it did before that animal attacked me. My left wrist looked like it was heavily bruised, yet when I touched it, I felt nothing. I didn't recall anything happening there either. I did spit out some darkish red blood when I woke up, but my body felt as good as it had ever been. None of it made any sense; those wounds and bruises, they should've at the very least left me bedridden for a week, another one just for me to be close to normal. Perhaps my father prayed for a quick recovery, and Allah granted it for him. I didn't want to think much about it, I was grateful, and that was all that mattered. All that rest I got must've helped accelerate my recovery. It took another day for me to fully fall back into my routine of work around the house. After that, I went back to the village to restock our supplies. I took the three eggs the chicken had laid and walked to my horse, hoping to get a few pieces of bronze or maybe a piece of silver if I was lucky. As I got there, I felt there was something different about the air, the forest. For some reason, I felt as if there were eyes watching over me. The wind started to pick up, the air got colder, and I knew I wasn't alone. I looked over to the forest, and for a split second, I saw the girl. Her eyes focused on me like an archer watching their prey. I was about to go over when the branches shifted, and she disappeared. Was she really there, or was she a figment of my imagination? I walked over, and there was no trace of her, no footmarks, no trail, nothing. She couldn't have been there, right?

I started to head to the village. As I walked past its entrance, I heard my name yelled by a voice that was slightly deep but still from a young man. I turned to see Charles sprinting toward me.

"My God, I'm so glad to see that you're all right," Charles said with a big smile on his face as he squeezed the life out of me in a bear hug. He was completely out of breath as he let me go, probably from him either working on his farm or sprinting to talk to me.

I remembered Charles being a scrawny, pasty child about the same height as me, close to five-six. Now I've grown maybe an inch or two, but he's grown like a tree, gaining at least half a foot, and that wasn't the only thing that changed. He'd clearly been working on the field with his body built like a skinny statue, his skin was soaked with the sun, looking practically orange. He went from a boy with barely any hair on his face to a man with a thin beard. As much as it weirded me out, he'd become quite the attractive man. Never thought about him like that, but six years was a long time, and we've both changed during that period.

"Glad to see you too, Charles. It seems like it's been a lifetime since we last spoke," I said to him, a small smile on my face.

"Something like six years. God, you've grown so much. How's your back and throat?" he responded with genuine concern in his voice, his right hand covering his eyes from the sun, the left reaching out to my back. I had forgotten he wanted to hear from us when I made my recovery.

"I'm doing much better; I just needed some rest," I said as I touched my neck. The pain was practically gone, yet it still felt stiff, as the same could be said about my back.

"I'd say. I thought he broke your neck with how purple it was, and your cheek was messed up badly. It's a miracle you're still here," Charles said as he lightly touched my face, immediately pulling his hand away once we locked eyes together, then gave an awkward laugh.

"Ha-ha, oh no, it's going to take a lot more than that to take me down," I said as I puffed up my chest in cockiness and bravado, immediately putting it down to laugh with Charles as he giggled at it too. "But I just wanted to thank you for helping me and my father out. I really appreciate it." I couldn't tell due to how orangey-red his face was, but it looked like he was blushing, which certainly boosted my self-confidence. He started to scratch his head and avoid eye contact with me, but his smile—his big, goofy smile—was still there.

"Aw, it's no problem. When I heard your father yelling for help, I couldn't let it go on deaf ears. I know we hadn't really talked in a while, but once I heard his cries, I had to help you," he said, slowly lifting his head up to look into my eyes. His little giggle was gone, but the smile was still there.

His smile, that look he was giving, one of care and love, like his world was right in front of him. It felt like the air was new, the trees felt greener, the plants bloomed into a vibrant life. I felt trapped in this dark world, with only my father, but Charles... It took a second for me to notice that I started to blush as well. I looked away from him for a second to regain my composure, but then, all the color, all the fresh air, all the life left me. I saw a force of about twenty men heading toward my house, with Louis leading them.

"Oh no," I whispered with fear crippling my voice, my hand covering my mouth. Everything started to die in front of me; the trees turned to black soot, the flowers lost their pedals and their stems shrunk. The man I killed must've worked for Louis; what other reason could that brute have to be heading to my home, to my father. Each breath I took was a struggle, as if my lungs were being squeezed. It took the sound of two horses neighing at each other to break my trance. I turned around, confused, to see Charles on one of the horses, offering me the other one.

"We got to go; your father could be in danger," Charles said to me. His smile disappeared; his face was one of resolve. Perhaps he had thoughts of concern but didn't let them shine through his stoic face. The waves of fear sunk below me as I found the courage to bury the emotion and grab the reins from Charles.

It was about a five-minute ride to my home, but it felt like my entire life passed by during that journey. Why head to my house? How could Louis know *I* killed his man? Did he even think that ass dead? All these thoughts and terrors reigned over me like it was the light from the sun. I turned my head to Charles, and for that second, the anxiety disappeared, but new concerns rose. Why was he doing this? He already saved my life, why risk his own for me, some girl he hasn't talked to for the last six years? It's one thing to help me when it's something simple like carrying me home and helping my father. It's another to side with me against Louis. Louis already had some sick fetish seeing me squirm; the second he learned or accused me of killing that donkey, we were as good as dead. We'd be branded as *traitors*, the one thing he probably hated more than those who worship the old gods. He'd already hung five people this year for their treason, what was three more? Perhaps it was out of the kindness in Charles's heart. Maybe he did care for me that much. I know selflessness was in short supply, but perhaps Charles wasn't like that. I thought for a second. If the shoes were reversed, would I do it? I tossed that thought out my head. Now wasn't the time for these philosophical debates. That was the least of my concern.

As we reached my house, I saw the men surrounding the front porch, yelling and screaming curses at someone. It was coming alive. I knew who they were yelling at, but I held out hope that perhaps I was wrong. I jumped off my horse and ran right into the scuffle, pushing through the crowd. And I saw my worst fear—my father being beaten senseless by Louis. I didn't hear their yells. I couldn't feel the wind or the ground, I only felt my insides turn, my heart stop, and my lung compress in on itself. My father's thobe was covered with his own blood and dirt. I counted at least two of his teeth lying on the ground. His nose was smashed beyond recognition, and his face was covered with deep gashes coming from the armored fist of Louis.

"Stop it! Leave him alone!" I screamed at the top of my lungs. I could feel my stomach settle down, my lung grasping for the air it needed to let out that primal roar. The fear left me; all I had was this flame in my gut. This anger, it pulled my focus to solely Louis, everything else was gone in my eyes, all I could see was him. The howling and cheers died out as I presumed they stared at me. Louis was still swinging away at my father's face, who looked only at me with his blacked eyes, but eventually, Louis turned around toward me with a sick, perverted smile.

"Hello there, my *querida*," he said, calling me "dear" with that vile look on his face, hands still holding onto my father's clothes.

"What the hell do you think you're doing here?" I said with my teeth clenched so hard, I could've ripped up a piece of silver with it. My fists were clenched, and I was taking short but powerful breaths through my nose as my body boiled with rage.

"I was looking for one of my men, Roger. He seemingly stumbled his way out here," he said as if it was his noble duty, standing up and looking down at me. "Once I heard what happened to you in the forest, I put two and two together. Did he hurt my little *angel*?" he said mockingly as he walked toward me, his smug appearance still on his face. He reached his hand to my cheek, and I immediately smacked it away from me. I heard the soldiers grab their swords, prepared to cut me down in an instant, only waiting for the order. Louis looked at his hand and smacked me across the face with a swift slap, right where *Roger* punched me. He obviously didn't like my act of *treason*. I fell to the ground and tasted the blood in my mouth. The slap reignited the pain in my cheek. Charles rushed up only to face five blades right next to his throat.

"Don't worry about me!" I yelled toward Charles, wiping the blood off my mouth. "Get out of here, now!" He nodded his head as he started to run back to his horse. Perhaps he'd get help, but I wouldn't have him die for me. Still on the ground, I turned over to see Louis was standing right on top of me. His smile had twisted into a scowl.

"So, this is the thanks I get. I protect you and your worthless father, and you both repay me with disrespect and lies," he said with the temperament of a child, angry and out of control, while walking to my father. "You won't admit to your treason, and your father worships a false god. I can tolerate your stupidity, but believing in *Allah* and not me is something that needs to be dealt with," he said as he kicked him in the gut. I saw my father spit blood out of his mouth while he rolled in pain. I immediately moved to help him, but Louis moved just as quickly, placing his iron boot on my back, pushing me to the ground as I tried to get up.

"Your man tried to rape and kidnap a child along with me! I wasn't going to let that happen, damn your rules and your *mercy*!" I screamed at him, trying to keep my face from submitting to the dirt.

"If he wanted to sleep with you, you should've been a good girl and realized your place, peasant. You and that child should've realized the honor he would've bestowed upon you," Louis said in a vile voice as he grabbed my hair and pulled my head up. "Who knows, he might've given you a true blessing and put a boy in that stomach of yours. Clearly your father needs one if he's stuck with *you* protecting him," he whispered in my ear as he lifted me up.

"You and your father have spit in the face of everything me and my men stand for. Is that how you repay Louis the Bold?" he said as we got face to face, showing off his disgusting, yellow teeth. I turned my face as his stench nearly knocked me out, trying to break free from his grasp but to no avail. Without thinking, I spat the blood he forced me to spill right into his face and gave him my own scummy smile.

"You're bold, all right, so bold that you're scared of an old man and his daughter," I said with anger and ferocity in my voice, staring right in his eyes as he wiped the blood away. The town all knew Louis was a gutless coward, using his overwhelming manpower to keep control. Yeah, he could fight, and he's killed some of his men who tried to overthrow him, but we all knew that if he didn't have their support, he'd be dead a long time ago. I knew he was going to kill me, but I wanted him to know how I felt about him, how we *all* felt about him. He practically growled at me like a wild animal as he threw me right next to my father and pulled out his blade, Dragon's Bane. Such a stupid name for a man who'd piss his pants if he saw the real beast.

"You want to show me disrespect? That's fine, your father was going to die for his actions, but now I may as well kill you too," Louis said as he pointed his sword in my direction, that sadistic smile returning. I glared at him, preparing myself for what came next when suddenly, someone threw a sword toward me. I guess these bastards were looking for some entertainment from me.

"Come on, you Spanish whore, pick up that blade and show us what you can do," Louis said, gesturing me to come over with his finger, taunting me.

I picked up the long blade. It was at least the length of my arm and thicker than the cloth I wore. It looked so fragile, yet it was heavier than I anticipated. I'd never used a sword before. My father and I thought it was useless to carry it around when a bow and arrow could do just as much damage from a distance, plus it was a lot heavier than a knife. I lifted it up with both hands and placed it right in Louis's face and stared right into his black, soulless eyes. My own eyes were filled with hate and bloodlust, so much that I knew it disturbed him. He looked slightly shocked that I would not only have the audacity to fight him, but I was fearless about it. It was a façade though; my body was trembling with fear, but I could care less about that, especially after I saw what he did to my father.

"Thought I was going to roll over and kiss your ass?" I said with anger in my voice. He trembled for a bit, but I realized it was all just a joke to him once that damn smirk showed up again. Our blades clashed twice, each hit nearly knocking the sword out of my hand, the third actually doing so.

"That would've been the smart move," he said as he took a swing right at me with his blade. I rolled out of the way and grabbed my sword from the ground.

"Oh, aren't you a feisty bitch?" Louis said, laughing like a deranged lunatic, continuing to chase me down. We clashed our blades three more times; each one I looked for an opening to take control. He found his opening with a swift and vicious headbutt, forcing me to stumble backward. I felt the blood leave my head, sliding down my face, off my nose, and into my mouth. Then, I felt his large boot kick me right in the gut, putting my ass to the ground, stripping the wind out of me as well. He took his blade and stabbed me in my right shoulder, piercing me to the ground. A blood-curdling scream came out of my body, all the pain rushed to my heart and head. It felt like a volcano was about to erupt and take me out. I looked at my shoulder and saw the blood drenching my blouse; my shoulder was all but numb. It took all my strength just to clench my fist and not pass out. Something within demanded for me to rise up; this wasn't my place to die. As he looked at me, laughing and taunting me, I nailed him with a swift kick right in his face and another kick right in his balls. I never saw a man's face go from happiness to pure pain and boiling rage so quickly. I screamed as he ripped his sword out of my shoulder, then I pulled myself up and grabbed the sword with my left hand, once again pointing it in Louis's face. The way he and the other men looked at me, they couldn't believe what they saw. My knees were about to buckle out from under me, and my chest was moving slowly up and down; I could barely take a breath without wincing in pain. Despite that, I was still ready to fight. The pain didn't matter, I wouldn't die on my back, I would die standing.

Louis ground his teeth and charged me, and for ten seconds, it was as if I was a prisoner of my own body, standing from afar, unable to do anything. I didn't tell my body to roll below his swing, I didn't tell my body to take my blade and, with all my might, stick it right through his black heart, piercing his heavily protected steel chest plate right through to his chest. I didn't tell my body to rip the blade out and cut his head off. In ten seconds, I killed Louis the Bold.

CHAPTER 3

Silence fell over the men surrounding me. I dropped to my right knee and used the sword to keep me up. As I dropped, a thick black-red sludge violently ejected from my mouth. My head was weary, my sight shifted, slowly dissipating, and half of my stomach was on the ground. It took a second, but I slowly realized what I had just vomited, blood. My eyes were stuck on the sickening sight, almost causing me to do it all over again. I couldn't grasp how it was even possible. He kicked me in the gut, but there was no way that caused this. I slowly lifted my head up and saw all of their eyes were on me. No one had made a move; their jaws were dropped, their faces spoke more words than anything they could've said, each either confused or shocked. I looked toward my father, and even through the blood-encrusted eyes, through his beaten and bruised face, he looked at me like he'd seen a monster. I felt a buzzing white noise in my ear. I could only hear my ragged breath pushing through my body. Any one of these cowards could easily kill me, but they did nothing.

Suddenly, I heard footsteps approaching us, not iron-clad steps or the stomps of horses racing down but the sound of leather boots hitting the earth. I turned to see a mob of people from the village rushing over, led by Charles. I didn't hear much from the men surrounding me, but their faces screamed panic and dread. I picked up a few words like "*escape,*" "*return,*" and "*Augustus,*" as they started to scatter off into the woods. None tried to take me or my father, fearing their own lives above all else. None moved the body of their fallen leader either, like the cowards they were, they fled once they lost. The mob arrived shortly after the men fled. I was still stuck on the ground, unable to move, unable to do anything. My sword was the only thing that kept me on my knees, otherwise, I'd probably be lying in my own vomit. I turned to their faces and saw looks of fear, shock, and awe. None were willing to take another step closer. There was about five feet between me and them; they stood away as if I had the plague.

"She needs help. Stop standing around!" Charles screamed as he pushed his way through the crowd toward me. I felt his warm hands around my left arm as he placed it around his neck so he could carry me. He lifted me up, and I clenched my jaw as a swift yet agonizing pain ran down my body. I closed my eyes, taking a quick breath through my nose to try and bury the pain. As I opened them, I saw my father was still on the ground, each breath sounding like it'd be his last.

"No..." I quickly muttered. "Don't worry about me. Go help my father," I pleaded to them. Charles looked at me with puppy dog eyes and nodded his head, putting my arm down and heading to my father's side. I joined him and got an up-close look at the beating my father got. His forehead was covered with bruises and cuts, his eyes were the size of large eggs from the swelling, three of his teeth had left his mouth, his nose was crooked beyond belief, and blood poured down his mouth and nose like a waterfall. I held onto his hand, at first tightly out of fear of losing him, but I eased up on it once I noticed he was grimacing in pain. As I looked at his beaten face, I felt water start to build up in my eyes. I couldn't let it out, though; I knew he needed me to stay strong. There was a look in his eye, behind the fear and the pain—a glimmer of hope and a sense of calmness. I bowed my head and closed my eyes, bringing his hand toward me.

"Please, God... Ya Allah, don't take my father from me, please save him and let him survive and recover from this beating," I pleaded as Charles and Victor helped him get back on his feet and took him to the house. I put my questions about Allah or a higher being to the side, my father needed my help. But just like six years ago, I couldn't do anything to save him. The men carrying him could do little to heal his body. I wanted all the pain he suffered to go away. I would've given anything to take his place. Yet there's only one Being that could save him, Allah. Now wasn't the time for questions or philosophical debates; all that mattered was my father surviving. All I could do was pray, pray that he would make it.

I could feel my chest tighten as I saw the people rush to his side as they placed him on his bed through his window. The thoughts I had carried with me, the selfish desires I buried deep in my mind and heart... How could I have ever thought like that? He was the only one who cared for me, and I thought it'd be better for him to be dead. I might've abandoned those thoughts as fast as they rose, but I still thought them, and I could never let that guilt go. I tried to wipe those thoughts away as I ran my one good hand down my face. I wouldn't let myself fall into this pit of despair. I *couldn't*. I knew it would consume and destroy me.

Without me saying a word, the people had already begun to help clean the destruction Louis had created. Despite their kindness, I felt their eyes circling back toward me, whispers being spread about how it was even possible for me to do this. Their whispers were justified. I couldn't explain it myself, either. How did I, a skinny girl, kill Louis, a *war-hardened* man? I dragged myself to my home. With each step, I gained a sliver of strength back, though I was still on the brink of death. As I entered, I felt someone place their hand on my left shoulder. I turned to see Pierre, who tried to hide the concern on his long face, placing a soft smile there instead. His presence, though adding some dread onto myself, loosened the tension in my chest. I felt safe. Knowing that all these people were here, knowing Charles was right there with my father, my breaths became stronger, my heart slowed down, my head wasn't thumping in pain. I felt a lingering sense of peace.

I turned my attention to my father as they did all they could to help him. They cleaned his wounds and wrapped up his broken body. Throughout the entire time, he didn't wake up, probably passed out from the pain, but he didn't scream, he didn't cry, nor whimper. He lay there, practically lifeless. I was not as strong, though, as they started working on my shoulder. I gritted my teeth, letting out a quick yelp as they wiped away the never-ending blood. Once cleaned, they put a tiny fire near the gash to make sure no germs would grow. The sensation I felt from the flames rose the hair on my body while a cathartic scream poured out of my throat. All the while, there was chatter around me, discussing Louis's death and speculating how it happened. *I* barely understood what happened; how could I explain it without sounding mad? *My instincts kicked in, and I pulled off a move with one arm that most men couldn't dream of doing*? I had no answers, none for myself and none for them either. It felt like a week had passed since I was in the town with Charles, but the sun's bright light slapping my face reminded me just how little time actually passed.

They placed a heavy set of cloth around my shoulder to control the bleeding should it open again. Once that was done, Pierre asked for everyone to leave so we could have our rest. I guess as the eldest, and with Louis dead, he would be viewed as the leader of the town. I know for myself, I've always viewed Pierre in that light, as our *true* leader, given all he knew and all Louis did to us. I'd never seen so many people at our home, nor had I seen the people ever rally like that. There wasn't even enough room for most of them to be inside; they spent their time outside, waiting for any sort of good news. They slowly disappeared back to their home, though as the day went by, people would bring us food as a gift, thanking me as they left. Pierre and Charles were the last ones in the house. As Charles got up to head back home, we stared at each other. He ran over and gave me a hug so tight he could've broken a rib if he held on. It felt nice though, after everything, to get that hug.

"Please get better," he said to me, tears building up in his bloodshot eyes, eyes that screamed concern and pain. He immediately left afterward, but his actions, his presence stuck on me like dirt underneath nails. I was at a loss of words for Charles. He could've abandoned me, left me for dead, but he returned with the village and was ready to die for me. I could feel a small smile on my face as I watched him run off. He truly did care for me, more than I could ever imagine.

Pierre and I walked over to my father to see the results of the village's work. Despite all the good they did for him, he still looked like hell. Part of me wanted to collapse by his side and plead for his life to be saved, but the sight of the smile on his face kept me composed. It wasn't a grin or a smirk; it was a simple, soft smile. It gave me hope that he'd be all right.

"Get some rest, dear. You're going to need it. I'll watch over Adam and make sure he's all right," Pierre said as he placed his arm on my shoulder, his long face still there. I nodded to him, and after I gave my father a kiss, I walked to my bed and immediately fell into a deep slumber.

I woke up by myself in a dark realm where all I saw was smoke on the ground and trees. I was in the same blue-turquoise dress as before, and my skin felt as if it would turn to that same color from the cold air. I had no scars on my body and felt no pain. I looked around the endless forest, trying to find anything, anyone. I knew this was like that last dream I had; perhaps this was the work of those spirits. This could be their way of reaching out to me, trying to tell me something, maybe that was what these dreams were. I started to wander through the forest, looking for any life. After a few minutes, I noticed someone in the forest, a young girl from what it looked like. Then it hit me: it was the same child from before, the one I saved. I ran over to her as she sat there, picking at flowers right next to her. As I got closer to her, the frigid air got warmer, the smoke thinned out, and the grass and trees slowly returned from the dirty blonde shade to a fresh shade of green. She turned over and had a smile on her face as she looked at me, waving like we were old friends.

"Hi there, Azul," she said with a youthful tone in her voice. The fear that consumed her face and the foreign tongue she spoke with was gone. It was like she was a new person. My mind wondered what had happened, how she was here and what happened to her after that pig attacked us.

"Kid, where are you, where have you been, why can I understand you?" I rambled off to her, my breath struggling to keep up with my thoughts. I could see a little giggle pop up on her face as I talked.

"Yeah, I'm sorry about that," she said while scratching the back of her head. "I'm right by the river next to your village. I'm not sure what you'd call it, but it's not too far from you."

She must be talking about the Garonne River. It's the closest river near me. Now that I looked around the region, it became more clear that we were there now. I could hear the river flowing far off from us, the cries of animals that surrounded us became more clear, like they were always there, but my attention took it out of my mind.

"I don't understand. What happened to you, what happened to me?" I asked her. I could tell she was holding out on me—the smile, her demeanor. She was too calm for my suspicion.

"I saw what happened to you, and I didn't want to disturb your sleep, so I figured it would be easier for me to talk to you in your dreams. I wanted to thank you for saving my life," she responded as she stood up, holding the flowers out to me as a gift. Irises and Lilies, each one filled with life and color. My mind was so stuck on how pretty they were, I nearly forgot my concern toward the girl. I turned my head to her, mouth agape trying to understand what she said.

"Wait, how could you possibly enter my dreams? That's impossible," I said with my eyebrows raised, trying to understand. Again, all she could do was scratch her head and laugh in a nervous tone.

"It's a long story. To be honest, I'm not sure how I could explain it to you. Tell you what, come by this river when you're ready. I'd be more than happy to explain anything you want," she said as she started to walk away from me. The world started to lighten up. I looked down and saw the dress slowly reverting back to my bloodstained clothes. I could tell my time was nearing.

"Wait, I don't even know your name?" I yelled toward her as she started to become smoke, reaching for her.

"It's Sadiq," her voice echoed back to me as a light flashed in front of me and returned me back home.

I woke up in a cold sweat, woozy and still drained. I looked down at my hands and saw the flowers were gone. I looked out the window to see the blue sky shining over us, though the sun must've just risen since I couldn't see it. I touched my shoulder and felt the dried-up cloth that was supporting it. It felt like the wound had closed itself up; the pain was still there but far better than where it was before I slept. My stomach no longer felt shattered, but my side hurt like someone was squeezing on it. I looked at my left arm, and the scar was still there. It looked as if it was old dark brown leather that'd been left in the heat, cracking under the pressure.

I put on my brown cloak to get warm and walked out of my bed to the living room where I saw Pierre sitting outside, drinking some wine he brought over. He knew that my father hated having wine in his house, what he viewed as his own mosque. I grabbed a loaf of bread someone from the village left us, probably Victor. I poured a bowl of chicken stew for me and Pierre and walked outside.

The first thing I noticed was that my front yard was fixed up after Louis's gang destroyed it. The gate for the animals was fixed, my father's bench was replaced with a new one. It must've been the villagers who did this. The thought of their kindness brought a smile to my face. He placed a second chair out there as he sat on the bench and stared into the forest. He turned his head to see me out and then turned it when he started to talk to me.

"Good morning, Azul. How are you feeling?" he asked politely as he put down his drink.

"Been better," I said as I stuffed my face with some of the bread while accepting a plate of two hard-boiled eggs he must have made. "How's he been?" I pointed behind me to my father's room.

"He's doing well. He has been asleep like that this entire time," he quietly said, taking a sip of the wine and staring at the forest, mesmerized by the sight of it.

"That's good to hear," I said as I sat down at the table. "I wouldn't know what to do if he died."

"Well, I know there's something we need from you," Pierre said, turning his body to fully face me. His face looked tensed up like he was worried about something. He took a deep breath and continued to speak. "With Louis dead, his men have fled the village. While that's great for us, we're now defenseless. We need someone to step up and lead our defenses, and I think you should be that person."

I looked at him in shock. My mouth, filled with mushed bread, eggs, and wet chicken, was left agape. Bits of my food actually fell out of my mouth. It took me a second to actually close my mouth, but his idea still hadn't registered in my head.

"What?" I said, dumbfounded. "Why me?"

"I just said why—we're left defenseless, we have no one who can protect us, and you singlehandedly killed Louis. I don't think there's anyone else who we can put in that role," he responded, his face becoming less stoic and more animated. A good reason, and one I should've expected. It made perfect sense. Before the rise of the empires and kingdoms, Pierre told me tribes usually followed the strongest and wisest. Once the Dragon arrived, rumors spread of small groups throughout France being ruled by tribal leaders. Most likely the rulers weren't the wisest, the oldest, or the most beloved. They were the people who could defeat any opposition. Despite the rationale, there was still this ulcer in my stomach at the thought.

"There's an entire village of people you can put in that role. I can't. Why not ask Victor or one of the other men, or someone who actually interacts with the people besides occasionally buying food?" I replied, not looking at Pierre. I didn't want to go into my fears, why I truly didn't want that position. The responsibility was one thing, but how could I accept it when the one person I did all I could to protect was nearly killed on my watch? I knew if I looked at Pierre, he'd get me to spill it out.

"No one in that town can do what you did. We've lived under Louis's rule for nearly eighteen years. You think you're the only one who hated him? He was a spineless meathead, but none of us could've touched him, until you somehow killed him," he said, waving his hands and nearly spilling his plate.

"It was dumb luck," I retorted, glancing over to him and then down at my food as I saw him look at me.

"Was it?" Pierre responded, his eyes still on me. *Was it*? I remembered my dream, my fight with Roger. Dumb luck would've saved me once, not against Louis as well.

"Azul, we need you to do this. You have no idea what could happen to us if we're left unopposed. Why are you fighting this so much?" He put his hand on my shoulder. I turned my face to see his, a face with the muscle tightened up, but not by stress. It was wrapped in a sense of dread and anxiety. Like my choice would decide his fate.

"Why?" I whispered aloud, still looking at Pierre. I could feel my shoulders about to give out on me from all the weight on them. *How can he not see it*, I wondered to myself. I took a breath and continued. "Just look at my father, and you'll see why," I said as I got up from my chair to get away. I could hear Pierre get up, placing his items down, but I had no interest in continuing this discussion. I wanted to be with my father, the man I failed to protect, the man who gave his all for me, and I couldn't do the same. The last family I had left in this world.

"Azul, you can't blame yourself for what happened to your father," Pierre said as he placed his hand on my shoulder. He turned me around to face him. Had it been anyone else, I probably would've pushed their arm off, but I couldn't do that to him. "You had no idea Louis would come. But you have a responsibility. You're easily the strongest out of us. We can't deal with what's out there without you." I removed his hands from shoulder, holding onto my wounded arm's elbow, thinking over what he was saying.

"And what's out there, Pierre?" I replied to him, a bit of sass in my tone.

"Men worse than Louis, no doubt. Once they hear from those men Louis is dead, we'll be ripe for the picking. We need you to lead our protection," he said with conviction in his voice, his eyes shooting daggers into my own. He was as serious as I'd ever seen him.

"I can't, Pierre, my father needs me. He's all I have left. I failed him before; I can't again," I coldly stated, my arms tucked into my side, head turned to the side, away from him, after I made my claim. "I'm sorry, I just can't."

Pierre shook his head in acceptance. "Well, I'll let the village know how you feel. I do hope you change your mind, Azul," he said as he went to his horse to head back home. As I started grabbing the plates and cups to bring them back inside, I heard Pierre call my name as he got on his horse, staring down at me. "I'm not sure what has convinced you that you're the reason he's like this, but I want you to know that I think you've done a fantastic job with your father. He's very lucky to have a selfless daughter like you." With that, he rode off to the village.

I felt a sting in my heart and eyes when he said that, like those kind words were daggers shot at me. Yet I questioned it; was I truly selfless, was my father lucky to have me? He might've been dead if it wasn't for me, but he wouldn't be in this position if I had done more to protect him. Was I truly selfless when I demanded information from my father, when I controlled everything in our life without bothering to talk with him about it most of the time? Would a truly selfless daughter even think that her father dying would be better for them? I don't know. What I did know was I wouldn't leave my father, not until he was healthy, no matter the situation.

I moved everything back inside and sat next to my father. His wounds had recovered nicely during his rest, though one could tell he was in a fight if they looked at him. "How did we get here, Father?" I said in a low voice, holding onto his hands. I gave it a quick kiss and then spent a few minutes taking care of the house, along with my father, who was comfortably sleeping. I changed from my blood-stained and dirty clothes into a blue blouse and black pants. The day went by fast. I spent most of it sitting by his side, leaving only to briefly eat and feed the animals outside. As the day turned into the night, I heard a knock on the door. I went outside to see Charles, who, upon seeing me, immediately hugged me.

"Oh, I'm sorry. Did I hurt your shoulder?" he said right after the hug, backing up just in case he actually hurt me. His face went from pure joy to concern in a second. *Such a kind man*, I thought to myself.

"No, no, don't worry about it. My shoulders healed up quite nicely," I replied with a bit of a chuckle as I removed the cloth on it, much to the surprise of Charles.

"Yesterday I could see right through it! How did this happen?" Charles asked like a curious child. I started to respond, but I stopped myself and thought for a moment about what I'd say. I didn't take too much time, but his face went from curious to confused.

"I have no idea," I quietly replied. I didn't want to go over what had happened to me with Charles—or anyone, for that matter. I didn't even know what happened to me.

His face was still stuck on that confused look. After a few seconds, he simply shrugged his shoulders and put his arm on my shoulder.

"Doesn't matter; you're safe and healthy. That's all that matters," he said with a goofy grin on his face, going from ear to ear. His joy brought a smile to my face too.

"Thank you, Charles. It wouldn't have been possible without you. How is the village doing?" I asked as I sat down in the kitchen, gesturing my hand to tell him to sit too. He took a seat and then a deep breath, exhaling quite loudly before he continued to talk.

"Well, that's why I'm here, Azul. We've been discussing what's next with Louis dead. There were plenty of discussions and nominations, but we came down to a vote," he said, taking a moment to seemingly think of what to say. He wrapped his hands together and put them to his face like he was praying, only for him to run his hands down his face. "And we voted you."

"I know you guys want me to lead, but I already told Pierre I won't," I responded quickly, confused. There was no reason for them to vote for me; I had already declined the option.

"Azul, Pierre asked you to do it. Only after this vote did we choose you," he said, his face long and tone depressed. My face was stuck in that confused position, mouth once again open, eyebrows raised. I shook my head to come back to reality and looked at Charles again, still a sad look on his face.

"Hold on. Didn't he tell you I wasn't going to do it? How could you vote for me if I already rejected it?" I asked with a slight hint of fury in my words. I could feel my face start to get more red with anger, my nostrils were flaring as I took quick, harsh breaths.

"He did, but we still felt you're the only one who can and should do it," Charles replied, trying to keep me from losing my temper, placing a hand on my shoulder.

I couldn't believe Pierre. It's one thing to ask, but it's another to not respect my wishes and convince the entire town to side with him. I stood up and walked to my window to try and compose myself. I took three deep breaths, each one more soothing than the next. I turned around to see Charles sitting there, waiting on me.

"Azul, we all know you killed Louis. Luck or not, you did it. Even with Pierre telling us you rejected his offer, who else could we look at but the one who killed him?" he said, standing up and slowly walking to me as he spoke. Once he was done, we were about two feet apart, but it felt like he was a hundred feet from understanding me.

"Is that why you're here, to convince me to accept the role?" I asked condescendingly, arms tucked into my sides, glaring at him. His long face came back, and sadness ran through it.

"I don't want to do this, Azul, but I think you know I wouldn't do this if I didn't truly believe in you," he answered back quickly to my sarcastic quip. I looked to the side, took a deep breath, and turned my head back to him.

"You may believe in me, but my father lies in that bed wounded because he believed in me. I couldn't protect him, the one person who put their entire life into my hands. I can't abandon my family again, not for anyone. I'm sorry, Charles, but I won't do it," I defiantly stated, staring right into his eyes. His face never flinched when I spoke to him. He stood there, cold and unmoving.

"Are you afraid of failing? That you won't be able to do what you did again? That instead of your father getting hurt..." he asked me, coming to my side, putting his hand on my left shoulder. I didn't respond, but my silence was deafening. The fear of losing everything, of losing my family, of failing, my body would practically shut down due to it. "We all fail, Azul, but that's why it wouldn't be just you. I know you rejected our offer, but I want you to come outside for a second," he replied in a soft voice. He offered his hand to me. I took it, and we went out of my home. When we got there, though the shadows covered it up, I could see what he wanted me to see: it was the entire village. What seemed like every single person was there, from Pierre to Victor, to Enzo, the blacksmith. All of them standing outside, waiting for me. Charles walked in front of me with his goofy smile on deck.

"I figured you'd refuse my offer, and no matter what kind words I say, you'll never believe that we believe in you. So I got everyone here to speak with you," Charles proudly stated, arms firmly placed on his hips.

I could feel my heart becoming heavier as Charles called on them to tell me their story, their relationship with Louis. I knew Louis was awful, a killer at heart, but hearing what he did to them, I realized the true burden I lifted for these people. I figured that those who couldn't supply him with his demands would be punished but some were taken as slaves, forced to work off their debt. Many were beaten and humiliated, some were even forced to do horrendous actions for his enjoyment. While my father and I stayed in our little area and dealt with Louis once every month, these people, *my people*, dealt with him and suffered at his hand constantly. I rarely talked to them, and whenever I did, I was too blinded by my focus to keep my father alive to truly notice the wrath of Louis. Maybe that's why I placed so much emphasis on protecting my father; perhaps I always knew what was happening and either didn't want him to suffer, or I never had the will to do more. No wonder they wanted me to protect them; I freed them from a monster.

"I want you to raise your hand if you were personally victimized by Louis," he yelled, turning to the crowd. I could see nearly everyone raise their hand; each one had a look of tragedy in their eyes.

"Raise your hand if you were relieved when you heard Louis was dead." All their hands stayed up, and my throat began to close up slightly. It was harder for me to breathe as my chest tightened.

"Finally, raise your hand if you believe in Azul as our leader and view her as family," he yelled out to the crowd, who all raised their hands and yelled back. I could feel my eyes start to water up; all these emotions were hitting like a blow to the gut. Charles turned around and came face to face with me. My body slowly relaxed, my chest loosening as he got near me.

"Each of these people, Azul, care for you. We know how much you care for your family, but we view you as family too. We're all we have, and we need you. You won't be alone, we'll be right beside you the entire way. We owe you that much," he said to me with a smile on his face. I hugged him and whispered a thank you into his ear. I was wrong to reject them. My family wasn't just my blood, it was those I cared for, those I wanted to see do well. I walked up in front of the crowd, all of whom were staring intently at me, all of whom had a determined look on their faces. I closed my eyes, took a deep breath, and began to speak to them, as their new leader.

"From the bottom of my heart, I thank all of you, for believing in me as your new leader. I promise you, on everything I hold dear, I'll do everything within my power to defend you and keep you safe from monsters like Louis," I yelled to the crowd, who roared with applause and happiness, chanting my name, the name of their new protector.

CHAPTER 4

The rest of the night went by quickly; as the villagers returned home, I stayed with my father. Eventually, whether it was due to sheer exhaustion or boredom, I fell asleep sitting next to him. I found myself awake in the wee hours of the morning, the sun barely up. I went out to stare at the sun rising over the trees, a new day as the new leader of the town. I looked down at the ground and thought about what had occurred recently, how my life had changed. I thought back to that dream I had, what that girl said to me. *Come by this river when you're ready. I'd be more than happy to explain it to you*. Perhaps she could explain why I was able to kill Louis, perhaps she could help me out. There could be a chance she was playing me, attempting to lure me away and be kidnapped. There was no guarantee that the forest was safe, and this girl entered my dreams, so it was clear she had some power. But if she was going to do anything, wouldn't she have done it when I was alone in that forest after Roger died, or even in my dream? There had to be more to the story than I knew.

I waited until Charles arrived at my home. I asked him to come by yesterday after I agreed to serve the people, to watch my father until I return, though I didn't mention where I was going. I simply stated I needed to head to the forest. Like the gentleman he was, he agreed, not questioning anything but instead offering me luck and safe travels as I headed off to find the girl.

I walked through the forest, to the Garonne River. It was east of where Roger attacked me, about a thirty-minute walk from my home. It had been a while since my last trip there to fish, but when I'd been there last, I felt something. Not what I felt in my dreams, but more of a spiritual peace within me. During that walk, I thought about what happened between my fight with Louis and Roger and how I survived them. Both occasions were life-and-death, and I was at the mercy of my instincts. It seemed like something outside of my control, some power, was acting out for me. A defense mechanism, a way for my body to protect me from threats. They also seemingly had some nasty ramifications as blood spewed out of my body violently on both occasions. Now that I've thought about it, my body always felt weaker after both occasions. I could barely stand or stay conscious after using those instincts. Perhaps that was my body rejecting the powers or just unable to hold up to the sheer willpower of it. Regardless, I had to find a way to control it if I wanted to survive as the protector of my village. My mind then wondered how I even got these powers in the first place. There were plenty of stories of people using dark arts and magic to gain powers, but that was all they were: stories. Could it have come from magic? A Dragon did fly across the sky; nothing was certain anymore. A blessing or a curse had been laid down on my lap, and it was up to me to decide which it was.

I finally reached the river, and it looked just like I remembered it, clear and blue like the sky. It was about ten feet deep, thirty feet wide, and so clean, I could actually see some of the fish swimming in the water. The wind felt so nice, and the water felt good as I took a handful of it to cleanse my face. I thought back to the memories I had here. The first one that came to mind was when I was just a girl, probably seven or eight years old, with my father. We spent nearly the entire day fishing, relaxing and enjoying the river. I remembered the fun we had as we swam in the water and the terrible fish puns he told. Even now, I giggled at his stupid joke where I reeled in a ten-inch trout and he acted like he didn't notice.

"Oh, sorry, I was deep in trout," he said as we died of laughter. I threw the trout at his face as I laughed at the joke. The muscles in my cheek and mouth were on fire from how much I was smiling. "Quite a gorgeous river, isn't it," a voice behind me said. I immediately pulled out my knife and pointed it right at the voice as I turned. I saw the girl holding her hands up, a nervous laugh coming from her. "Sorry," she said awkwardly as I put my knife down. The girl was wearing the same thing she wore that day I first met her. Now that I thought about it, every time I saw her, she looked the exact same. I looked around, seeing if there was any difference I could notice.

"This isn't a dream, right? You and I are here in reality?" I asked. I knew I had woken up, that I walked all the way over here. However, after all I'd been through, I wanted to make sure. She shook her head in agreement, her small smile turning to a glowing grin. I sat down next to the river, exhaling a deep breath and rubbing my hands across my face, staring down at the ground. Everything that had happened, all the changes and shifts, I didn't know where to start. My mind couldn't wrap around any of it as it made no sense to me. I took a deep breath and turned to her; she seemed perplexed by what I was doing, but her glow was still there.

"What happened to me, Sadiq? What happened during that fight with Roger, what happened to you?" I asked the child, each word holding a sense of tension and pain. She looked at me, and I could feel there was a sense of pity in her eyes. She sat down in front of me, took a deep breath, and began to speak.

"Azul, you have powers. They came alive when you fought that jerk," she said, so matter-of-fact, like the sun rising from the east to the west. My throat tightened, like a loaf of bread was stuck in it. The confirmation led to a rise of temperature in my body. Sweat dripped down my brow, and I wiped it as fast as I felt it.

"What powers; how could they *come alive*?" I countered, swallowing the wad of stress in my throat. She started to scratch her head, tilting it slightly to her right. Her face was scrunched up like her nose had been hit with the foulest smell in the world.

"It's hard to explain. The powers come from oneself, their soul," she replied, touching her heart. My hand slowly worked itself to my chest, feeling the rapid beats coming from my heart. As I touched it, my heart shifted from the rapid flap of a bird's wings to a cool river flow, slow and constant. "From your soul, depending on your control, your powers can do whatever you want it to," she continued.

Whatever I want, I said to myself. She nodded her head in approval. "Anything, from strength," she stated as she tried to flex her biceps. "Brainpower," pointing to her head, "to whatever you can think of, it's all yours!" she yelled with the joy of a child receiving a present, opening her arms to the world.

"But I have no control of it. How was I able to use it, and how did it even come to me?" I asked, feeling much calmer. My soul seemed relaxed by Sadiq and her attitude, which felt like a sun's ray cutting through a dark forest.

"Your powers were protecting you, Azul. It probably came out instinctually. In terms of where they came from, I don't even know where to begin." Sadiq shrugged her shoulder. "I can tell just from looking at you, your power is radiating from your soul. It's nothing I've ever seen." I thought about the fight, the two killing blows, how I had no say in the moves I made. I touched the skin on my left hand, the one that was dirty and scarred. It was still dry and leather-like, it hadn't improved at all; it might've gotten worst. My mind ran back to that sight of black blood I puked after Louis. Was my body rejecting these powers? Were these powers killing me?

"Is there any side effects?" I asked, my voice rattled, concerned about my well-being.

"I've never faced any myself, but you're the first I've ran into that has these powers, Azul, that's why I ran toward your place. I could feel some faint warmth in your direction, something telling me that I'd be safe near you." The joy from her voice and her smile again relaxed me. For whatever reason, I was at ease here, in her presence. Yet her answer brought up more questions.

"What about you? If you have these powers, why did you need help, why can we speak the same language now and not then?" That question changed her perspective; she went from visible joy to a look of concern, her smile left for a long face, wrapped with a deep thought.

"I was afraid, so I was speaking my native tongue to you, sorry about that," she replied, looking down at her hands, which were constantly moving. I noticed her hands were a bit darker than her arms, and she kept trying to hide that from me, even sat on them after a bit.

"Sadiq, you don't have to answer my questions if you don't want to, I understand," I said, reaching my hand out to her to help her feel better. Her face reverted back to her joyful look, her eyes brimming with happiness as tears began to swell up. She briefly wiped them away and grabbed my hand with both hers, squeezing it tightly.

She had to be going through a lot herself, being out here, alone, no one to protect her, no one to play with her, no one to give her love and support. She looked like she was ten; I could only imagine the horrors she must've seen to be here. I couldn't force her to talk, no matter my curiosity.

"If you'd like, you can live with me at my home," I suggested. She shook her head no while still holding on, still keeping that joy on her face.

"Thank you, but I'm happy living here, in nature, away from all the chaos. It's where I've lived my whole life, and as great as it would be to live with you, I'd rather stay here."

I nodded my head in agreement. "Please, though, try and stay close so I can help you if you're threatened by anyone." This time, as I spoke, I put my other hand on hers.

"I will. That jerk, Roger, you said, he just happened to come around while I wasn't paying attention in the river. I'm not great with my powers, so I needed help, hence why I came to you," she said in a sour tone, looking down. "Doesn't matter now. I wanted to help you find a way to channel your powers." Her attitude shifted to a cheerful glee as she let go of my hand and returned to her spot. "So, in order to reach your powers and use them at will, you must reach your soul. At that point, it becomes like a river, flowing through you. I find the easiest route is to reach peace within yourself," she said, taking slow and deep breaths to calm herself. She pointed at her body to show how it'd work, going from her chest, following her veins all across herself. "Once you control it, you can take it anywhere."

"Reach your soul, peace within yourself," I said to myself. I closed my eyes and started to only focus on myself, the sounds of water slowly disappearing from my ears as did the wind and chirping of animals. My thoughts and fears slowly faded from my memory, the faces of the people within my town disappeared. I only saw the forest from my dream, no light around me, only blackness and trees. The darkness started to shift slightly, turning more sapphire. I could feel something within myself slowly changing; my body felt stronger than ever, my shoulder felt as fresh as ever, my feet, sore and cut up, felt rejuvenated. The sapphire color turned brighter as I kept my focus; it felt like I was drowning in it, overwhelmed by it all. It turned bright white, and I felt like I was ripped from the light, pulled by my shoulders.

I found myself awake back in the real world, staring at the ground from my hands and knees. My forehead was drenched in sweat; my lungs were so desperate for air, I was gasping for anything. All the while, there was a rumble coming from my stomach and something rising through my throat. I spat out a bit of that dark blood from my throat. After a bit, my lungs and heart slowed down, returning to normal. I looked up to see an astonished yet seemingly proud Sadiq.

"That was unbelievable, Azul. You grasped so much power, I—" She cut herself off as she shook her head, wiping the look of awe on her face. "I've never seen so much raw power."

As I looked around, I noticed slight differences around us. The light had changed, going from crystal clear to autumn red, the sun, which sat in front of me, had turned to my back.

"How long was I doing this for?" I gasped to her, still reeling from it.

"Most of the day, you controlled it for about fifteen seconds though."

My eyes grew wide, and I immediately caught my breath. I spent the day trying to harness it, and I only held onto it for fifteen seconds? But those seconds, I felt like I was untouchable, like I did when

I fought Louis. I only had a grasp of it, I couldn't move, I couldn't run or fight, I might've had a finger on it, but that was enough.

"I can do this," I confirmed to myself. Acting on its own to save my life was one thing, but to summon it at will, even if I was only able to contain it for a few seconds? I would probably be able to defend those I care for. My face lifted in joy. I looked over to Sadiq, who was beaming with happiness. She nodded her head in agreement as she hugged me. Her love only added more joy to me as I hugged her back.

"You'll be an amazing protector, Azul," she said as she let go. "Thank you for everything." I giggled a little bit after she said that.

"Thank *me*, I should thank you too. I'd be clueless to figure any of this out without you."

"Perhaps, but you saved me, and for that, I'll do whatever I can to help you out," she said.

I once again offered my hand to her. "As will I, Sadiq. I'll try to visit whenever I can." Smiling, she shook my hand and pulled us both up from the ground.

I started to grab my tools to head back home. As I prepared to leave, I looked around for one last goodbye, but she was gone. As if she was the wind, here for a while but always moving.

As I started the journey back home, the only thing I thought about were *these gifts*. I ran through everything I had done that could've led to me gaining these powers, how they could've landed in my lap. Maybe this was a miracle from Allah, much like what was done for Musa, or Moses as others called him, and Muhammad, peace be upon him. Perhaps it was his way to counteract the beast, though I chuckled at the thought. I highly doubted Allah or whoever ruled over us would act now rather than when the Dragon arose. But what else could've given me these gifts? Maybe it was magic, a ludicrous thought but in a world where a Dragon reigns supreme, who's to say? Slowly my mind stumbled to Sadiq, who she was and her story. She was obviously hiding something, but I wasn't sure what it was. Perhaps it was for the best. She did tell me how to use my powers. She went to my father to grab his attention after Roger. I didn't believe she was trying to get me killed, rather she had her own life and secrets. Was it so wrong for her to have that?

By the time I arrived home, the sun was just about to set, yet if I looked up, I'd be able to see the moon in the sky. I noticed the animals were noisier than usual. I didn't think much of it as I wanted to eat and sleep. Once I entered my house, I was taken aback by the sight before me. It was as if a king's ransom was left for me: a bushel of fresh fruits and vegetables and six loafs of fresh bread. I turned to look outside to see a dozen chickens, cows, and goats in the backyard, and so much more. My hand went to my mouth in stunned awe. This had to be the work of the village. A thank you, I presumed, for accepting the position as protector. The gift that grabbed my attention was the silvery-blue set of armor that sat by its lonesome to the side. The armor gleamed in the little sunlight remaining like a diamond Pierre would describe. The blue shade gave it a unique look; I figured most knights' armors were usually just silver or white. The steel looked like it was freshly made from the highest quality of steel I had ever seen. No cracks, no dents. Though I lacked knowledge in forging, someone would have to be blind to not know how good this armor was.

I looked down to the right and saw there was a scabbard that had a sword in it, turning my curious joy into overwhelming excitement. I pulled the blade out, and the shine on the stainless steel forced me to squint my eyes for a second. I moved it out of the sunlight, and I got to truly revel in its beauty. The steel looked freshly forged and had a gleam to it that would make a hardened blacksmith cry from the beauty and perfection of it.

"Beautiful, isn't it?" I heard from behind me. I quickly turned around and pointed my blade in the face of Charles, who went from a goofy smile to a look of fear. He immediately put his hands in the air. "Whoa... Guess I should've said hi before walking in," he said with a small chuckle. I started to giggle as well as I lowered the blade.

"Sorry about that, just a bit jumpy."

Charles squinted his face and raised his hands up in a quick shrug. "Oh really, I never would've guessed that with the shocked look on your face and the blade in mine," he said with a grin.

"Ha-ha," I said to Charles, rolling my eyes. "All this from the villagers?"

"Yep, they've come over throughout the day dropping stuff off," he replied, waving his hands across the room.

"How's my father been?" I quickly asked him, looking toward his room.

"He seems to be doing a lot better today. He actually woke up..." Charles began to say, but as soon as I heard his words, I immediately turned my attention toward him.

"He did?" I responded, sprinting to his room. I opened the door with a massive smile only to be bitterly disappointed to see he was back asleep. Charles placed his hand on my shoulder in support. I turned to see his calm face looking at me too.

"He was awake. I gave him some bread and water and then he went back to sleep," Charles whispered to me. I gazed at my father with a sense of relief in my heart.

"At least he's improving," I said to Charles. I glanced at his freckled face, his goofy smile with a gap between his two front teeth, his brown eyes. Knowing that he was here to help me brought me a sense of calmness. I wrapped my arms above his shoulders and hugged him. "Thank you so much, Charles. I appreciate your help."

"Of course, what are friends for, right?" I could hear the happiness in his voice. I hadn't talked to him in years before this week. We were close friends at one point, but I didn't know if we were still that or if we were more than that.

"Right. We're friends, and friends help each other, so if you ever need anything, please let me know," I conceded to him.

"If anything comes up, you'll be the first to know, *my lord*." He chuckled as he bowed his head like I was the queen of France. Neither of us could contain our giggles from the silliness of it. After we regained our composure, our eyes locked. I could feel my face begin to get a bit hotter, particularly my cheeks, and I saw he was too. My stomach started to get queasy, my heart banging on my chest, as I was unable to say anything to Charles.

"Well, I best be on my way. Bye, Azul," he flustered out of his mouth as he rushed out of the house.

Great, I thought to myself. That's exactly what I wanted to see; a guy I started to like running off like a chicken with its head chopped off.

I sat down next to my father and looked at his face, the small smirk still on it, the wounds that were healing at a snail's pace, how his hair had reverted back to its pale white color from the mixture of red and brown that coated it. I pushed his hair to the side and kissed him on his forehead and whispered for him to sleep well. As I got up to go to sleep, I heard some muttering words behind me. I turned around to see his groggy eyes begin to open, whispering my name. I sprinted right to him and hugged him, barely able to contain the joy and glee within me.

"Oh, Azul... my precious girl," he slowly said as he patted me on my back and chuckled. "Glad to see... you haven't forgotten your old man."

"Of course, Father. I could never forget about you," I said as I held on to him for dear life. I closed my eyes in relief. I could feel tears starting to build up and wiped them away. I knew, I knew if my life would end here, I'd die a happy woman. I didn't need anything other than this; all I wanted was one more moment with my father. After a few more moments of our embrace, I released him from my grasp and composed myself.

"How are you feeling?' I asked him. He still sat comfortably, unmoving and slow to react toward anything.

"Well... other than my back being crushed by your hug, I'm feeling better... how about you?" he weakly asked with a small smile on his face. Even after the beating he took and how long he was out for, he still cared about me over everything else. I scratched my head and took a deep breath.

"I'm fine, Father. As long as you're okay, I'll be good," I replied, gripping his hands in a soft yet firm grasp. It'd been a long time since I'd seen his eyes have a shred of happiness in them.

He softly placed a finger on my shoulder where Louis left me his farewell present and, in a faint and weak voice, said, "Even there?"

I delicately took his hands and gave them a soft kiss.

"Even there, Father. He can't hurt us anymore," I said as I placed his hand down on his stomach.

He closed his eyes with his lips grinning from cheek to cheek. It was clear he was still weak and needed to rest as much as he could.

"That's good to hear. I'm so proud of you, Azul... thank you," he said as he fell back to sleep.

He must still be severely hurt from Louis's actions. I went to the kitchen and grabbed him a plate of grapes and cut a piece of bread off and placed it right next to him so he could munch on it whenever he woke up. The food tasted fresh, like it was made today. As I walked into the living room, I stared at the armor, at its design, the coloring of it. It was mesmerizing. I imagined myself in the armor as I stared down men who dared to enter this town, *my town,* and imagined crushing them. I took the helmet off the suit. I could see my reflection in its blue tint. The color was the exact same as my eyes, sapphire blue.

I felt the heavy weight of the steel pushing my arm down, but even then, I felt this rush of power as I held it. I placed it back and went to train, as I knew the weight my shoulders carried. As the day turned to night, I spent my remaining few hours training my body to take the weight of my gifts. I would chop logs until my arms were so sore, they would barely lift themselves up. I would put all the logs I cut onto our sled and push it around, using the strength from my back and legs to move. It wouldn't matter what direction I went or for how long, just as long as I put my body through hell. Finally, before I went to sleep, I made the attempt to summon my gifts, reaching that inner peace. It took a few hours for me to find that peace, but I was still only able to crank out my strength for about ten seconds. Exhausted, I finally went to sleep, as I had a lot on my plate that needed to be taken care of.

CHAPTER 5

I woke up the next day to the sound of the chickens clucking at the top of their lungs. It wasn't too loud, but all their cries, along with the moos from the cows and shrieks of goats, were annoying enough to wake me up before the sun even rose. As I rose from my bed, I expected my body to still be racked with pain from my workout, yet I felt nothing. My arms were ready to fizzle away last night, today they felt stronger than ever. My legs, which would've been blown away like tree branches if there was enough wind, felt like the trunks of a great oak tree. Those precious seconds of control must've revitalized my body. I looked at my left wrist, the mark had stayed the same but the colorization of it differed. It went from a dark brown to a shade lighter. Improvement, perhaps?

I walked to my father's room to check in on him, but he was still sleeping like a baby. After that, I went outside to see our once cozy pen filled with eight new chickens screeching, two cows sleeping, and two goats' bleats. There really wasn't much I could do other than placing the chickens out of the pen and putting them in the backyard with our horses. They had plenty of space to run around and cluck. I'd have to make some new pens for the other animals at some point. I looked up at the sky and saw that neither the sun nor moon was up, yet I kept looking, taking its beauty in. The billions of stars splattered across the sky, the dark shade of blue that served as a canvas for them. A tilt of orange started to fly on top of the forest, meshing with the blue and creating a majestic sight. It was like a master painter was given the sky to work with.

As I went back inside, I saw the suit of armor in my living room. I realized I'd never tried on anything like this. I didn't know the first thing about suits or armor. I tried to put the helmet on, and the weight of it went straight to my neck. I wasn't able to hold my head upright nor keep it stable as I dropped it on the ground. I quickly looked toward my father's room to see if that woke him, but he was still asleep.

I pushed the armor set outside so I could try it on and let my father sleep in peace. The suit had a simple design; the arms and legs were connected to the chest through hooks on the edges of it. Putting it on was another question entirely. As I put the chest piece on, it nearly dragged me down. I had to use all my strength just to stay standing. I was able to get the armor for my arm on but couldn't get it connected, and there was no way I would be able to get the leg piece on too. I'd imagine I resembled a fat silver-blue pig in this suit. There was no way I could walk in this getup, not to mention fight in it. I tried to focus and reach my inner peace, but I couldn't even focus on it with all the weight on me.

I threw the armor down and just stared at it, contemplating what I could do with it. The armor on the arms and legs wasn't too heavy like the chest piece. The sky had turned from a crystal blue to a melancholy orange, the stars had disappeared, and the sun had risen from the horizon. I would take the armor to the blacksmith who made it when I was done with my chores; it's not like there was a rush.

I quickly fed the animals, attempted to milk the cows, cleaned up around the house, and prepared bread and beef for my father while also making a plate for myself and eating it. He was still asleep, but at least when he woke up, there would be food waiting for him. After I finished my work, some time had passed, and the sun had finally risen. Hopefully, the blacksmith would be awake when I got to the village.

The ride was quiet, and when I got there, most people weren't at the center. The few who were out waved at me and had giant smiles as I passed by. It still felt weird that to these people I wasn't just a fly roaming the town, I was practically their queen. I waved awkwardly at them with a small smile on my face and made it to the village's edge where the blacksmith was.

Each step my horse took, the ringing sound of steel smacking steel got louder. He must be hard at work. The blacksmith's armory was a small place, made completely of clay and stone. It did have a second floor, which was probably where he slept. The home was right next to Louis's tower, his base of operation. Most villagers ignored the watchtower as it was where Louis and his men would spend most of his time drinking, at least I certainly tried to.

As I got off my horse and knocked on his door, the noise of work came to a screeching halt. I heard a few footsteps to my right side, and I saw the blacksmith, Enzo, I believed his name was.

"It's you," he gushed, nearly choking up through the process. The man was small but bulky, having a thick, long, black beard to go along with his long hair, looking like a tiny bear. His face was covered with sweat and soot, his shirt blackened by smoke and his hair was greasy. His hands looked like thick brown gloves given how much soot and burnt marks were on them. Despite the dirt, I could see thick calluses on his hand and how massive they were. Clearly, he had been busy, yet he had a massive smile on his face.

"Hello, Enzo, do you mind if I have a moment of your time?" I politely asked, returning his smile.

"Of course, of course, you don't even need to ask, you can have anything you want," he said joyfully, quickly opening the door. The second I walked in, I felt the flames of his forge hit me like a punch to the face. The inside was filled to the brim with weaponry and armor, from swords and spears to steel helmets and leather tops.

"What can I do for you, my lady?" he asked me with a proud smile on his face, hands to his side.

"There's no need for you to be so formal, Enzo, Azul works for me. I'm not your lady or *queen*, I'm just a neighbor," I responded, scratching my head slightly.

"Sorry, I've been stuck in this mentality of ass-kissing due to Louis. It's tough for me to break out of it. He lived so close and always wanted more weapons and armor, his insufferable thirst for power was fueled by his love for intimidation. But the bastard is dead, and it's all because of you and for that, I'm indebted to you," he retorted, bending in a quick bow to me.

"You're indebted to no one; I did what I'd imagine anyone would do in my shoes," I said, placing my hand on his shoulder and looking into his eyes. The idea that this village owed me anything was laughable. If any of them had these gifts, I'd imagine they'd do the same thing. He gave a small smirk and took my hand off his shoulder.

"Azul, I appreciate your belief in us, but you don't need to lie. There's a reason Louis ruled with an iron fist for eighteen years here. Anyway, I imagine you're not here to just talk about Louis, is there anything I can do?"

"It's your armor. It's beautiful but takes away my speed, and I don't even have the strength to use it effectively. I'm protected, but that won't mean anything if I can't attack," I said to him, taking the helmet out and giving it to him. "Do you have anything that could protect me but let me keep my speed and mobility?"

He scratched his chin as he thought over our conundrum. He roamed across his workshop, opening a few cabinets to our right, looking for a solution. After a few minutes of searching, he finally returned and presented what appeared to be a thick black leather chest piece with two pieces of thin steel that squished it together like a dusty sandwich. He also brought a black leather top that would cover my arms, though not as thick as the chest piece.

"What do you think of this? The leather and steel may not protect you as well as that thick armor, but you'll keep your speed, and they should protect you a lot more than your regular clothes from quick swipes," Enzo said to me. I grabbed the leather, and I noticed the thickness of it and the durability of it. A sword could pierce it if driven down, but a swipe of a blade should be thwarted. There were plenty of scratches and marks on it, but it still felt fresh. I grabbed one of his arrows and slowly jabbed it so I would know how protective it was. It took my third jab to poke a tiny hole in it and even then, I was pushing a lot of force onto it. *Good,* I thought to myself. I put it on, and the heat from the forge grew from the leather, yet it was also opposite from the chest plate, thick yet not heavy.

"Yeah, this is perfect, I'm not weighed down, and I'm protected. Thank you, Enzo." I joyfully said to him, extending my hand to him to thank him. He gleefully shook my hand with that delightful smile on his face.

"You're welcome, my lady. You should be able to wear the arm and leg armor with this so you'll have complete protection. If you want, I could whip up some more thin armor for you?"

I slowly shook my head no in response. "You're too kind, Enzo. This works perfectly for me. Thank you very much." I left his workshop with my new gear on, looking to go back home.

As I got to my horse, a child no older than six ran up to me with Charles right behind him. The boy, who looked like a younger version of Charles, looked extremely distraught and like he had been crying; Charles's face was one of concern, like he'd seen a ghost.

"Azul?" the child barked through heavy breaths as he tried to fight through his tears.

"Yes, what's wrong?" I said as I bent my knees to look him in the eye.

"My dad is in trouble; he needs your help!" he wailed as he grabbed my hand and tried to drag me along. As I started to run with him, my mind raced to figure out what this child wanted with me. Why would his father want to talk to me?

Then it hit me. I was the protector of this village; he needed me to save his father or more gut-wrenchingly, save this village. As we continued to run, there was a feeling of sickness in my stomach. My hands felt clammy, my sight was getting less clear by the second, and my head felt as light as a feather. My heart was banging on my chest; every second it felt like it was getting stepped on. Each breath I took felt like it was my last as I started to suffocate. Suddenly, I found myself on my hands and knees, gasping for air. I was at the brink of death, just from the thought of protecting my village. What a stupid lie I told myself, that *I* could defend this village. Yet the second they needed me, my body gave in to the fear.

That fear started to build on top of itself, manifesting into my darkest terrors; me holding my father as he died, the village set aflame, the people burnt to ashes. I looked down to see my hands in chains as my hair was pulled up, forcing me to watch as they all suffered and perished. The last of the nightmare was when a hand pierced through my chest, holding onto my broken heart, and a set of red, purplish eyes staring at me, filled with anger and hatred. *I can't do this, I lied to myself and everyone here.* All the gifts in the world wouldn't change the fact that I was a scared girl, alone, weak, powerless. As my mind collapsed, I'd completely forgotten about the boy as he tried to pull me up from my left arm.

"Come on, Azul, my dad needs you," the kid whined to me. On my right arm, I felt someone trying to help me up softly, not as intense as the kid. I turned around to see it was Charles.

"Are you okay?" he whispered as I stared at his brown puppy-dog eyes.

The sickness in my stomach disappeared, my sight slowly came back to me, my heart and lungs slowed down, and my head returned to normal. The nightmares vanished from my mind, the chains were gone. I touched my chest to see it was fine. Just the presence of Charles reverted all my fear and panic. *I'm not alone*, I thought to myself. *I have Charles, I have this village.*

"Yeah, I'm fine," I said to him as I rose, my strength returning to my legs. We sprinted to the kid's house just outside the western edge of the village, practically a straight shot to my home. It wasn't too far from Enzo's home, but it felt like we ran across the entirety of France in that time. As we got there, we found a man outside with a gash on his head, with a woman cleaning it up, and a crowd starting to build around him. The man looked like he had been beaten badly with a massive black right eye and his nose and black beard covered with blood. As I got closer, the crowd started whispering my name, starting to split like I was

Musa and they were the Red Sea. I tried to ignore it as I focused on the man, whose face went from a pit of misery to a ray of hope.

"Azul, thank Jesus you're here," he said with a weakened tone, extending his hand out to me. I had noticed more people were more willing to show their religious beliefs since Louis died. I had seen a few crosses in the window of homes, even this man had a small cross around his neck. Perhaps it was Louis who kept their faith down, rather than the appearance of the Dragon.

"What happened?" I asked him as I took a knee right next to him, holding his hand lightly.

"Russell, Louis's second in command. He attacked me. I was fishing by the river, and when I was returning home, he and his men nearly killed me," he said, taking a moment to cough out some blood. "He told his men that they're coming for this town and to put your head on a spike tonight."

My stomach dropped; my fears had come true. How could I protect this village from the remnants of Louis's force? I had gotten lucky killing Louis; it was one-on-one combat. His men were dumbfounded when I did it. Now the rest of his men were coming here, fully committed to taking this town back. My mind raced through all the flaws I had going against me: I hadn't learned to control my powers, nor was I a hardened soldier of war, I had no experience planning a defense. My confidence was shot; I feared the worst, but I swallowed it away. I wouldn't show my feelings of fear, not in front of the people who believed in me.

"How many men were there?" I asked, clutching my fist tightly as my voice shook with fear.

"Twenty men, maybe more," he uttered. That wasn't too bad. I stood up and tried to look around the town, trying to make a plan. Their stares were practically daggers, piercing my false confidence and sanity. It was overwhelming, but I couldn't break down. One deep breath later, and my mind started to put a plan together.

"We need the whole town on alert; everyone needs to be ready to fight when Russell comes in," I commanded. "Where were you attacked? Which direction?" He slowly pointed north, in the direction of the tower. "All right, then that's where they'll most likely strike. Everyone needs to be there with either a bow and arrow or a sword so we can defend ourselves."

"What about you?" someone in the crowd asked.

Those words felt like a gut punch. I knew what I needed to do, but my mind thought of every possible way to avoid it. *No*, I thought to myself, *I can no longer be on the defensive, I took this task, and I must protect these people. I must do what's right. Fear may rattle my body, but I won't let it control me.*

"I will fight Russell myself and defeat him," I proclaimed with a sense of vigor and commitment that I hadn't shown since I took this role. The nerves disappeared, my heart slowed down, my breath, ragged and panting at one point, had regained composure.

"They'll probably come at night to get us at our weakest, but they won't know we're prepared. Anyone with a bow should be placed on the roofs facing the north side and those with a sword or a pitchfork will stand together right at the northern entrance and keep them out of the village. As long as we keep them at bay with our arrows and they don't get us from behind, we can beat them!" I screamed toward the crowd. Some nodded in agreement, yet there were many who were still, looking around for reassurance, still frightened by fear. I walked to the front of the house so I could see everyone there, so I could see their faces, and they could see mine.

"My people, I know you're scared, and you have every right to be scared! But if we don't act now, if we don't act to protect our village, Russell will force us back to the life we were in with Louis and no doubt punish us for betraying him! We have a chance right now to change our lives and the lives of those who'll follow us. I won't let that go because of fear. I'm just as scared as you are, but I won't let it consume me," I roared to the crowd. They started to rally behind my call. They believed in me; I could see it in their faces as they lit up. Their heads nodded in agreement. I saw one face, old and leathery with his skin, and a face that, other than the rose-red cheeks and nose, was as pale as a ghost. He shook his head in disgust, as if I wouldn't make my promise a reality, that he wanted us to fail. My face hardened with a look of determination as I glared right through the soul of that old man.

"If you think you're better off with Russell controlling your every move and with me dead, you can do nothing, but if you want your own life, your *own* town, then take these blades and join me!" I let out in a thunderous yell.

The crowd roared with excitement, ready to fight for their home. They started to rush home and grab their pitchforks, blades, bows and arrows, whatever could be used to fight. I saw a group head to Enzo's shop as he started to hand out blades, armor, arrows, bows, whatever he had that was sharp or useful. As the crowd dwindled, I noticed the old man was walking to his house. I didn't think much of it; he would neither help nor harm us from there. I walked to Enzo's shop as the roaring mob shuffled through the village. We passed the armor and weapons out and gave them to the people who had nothing.

Once the crowd started to die off and everyone was given something to fight with, Enzo helped make sure I was as prepared as possible. I wouldn't use the gloves or the helmet of the armor; I felt it was too heavy to make it worthwhile. He had a pair of dark blue leather pants and gloves I could use, both of which were better than what I had. The gloves were thin and allowed me to still have mobility while protecting me a bit if anything were to occur to my hands. The pants had a bit of steel in the leather, much like the leather top, it was just thick enough to take a grazing shot but thin enough to keep my speed. I wouldn't be able to take many hits, but I would dish out plenty. That was, if I was able to unleash my power. After I was set up, Charles barged into the armory.

"We need to talk," he snapped toward me, his voice as stern as it had ever been. "Alone." He stared right at Enzo with a stone face. Enzo looked at me with concern in his eyes, but I patted him on the shoulder and simply told him, "It's all right; help the others outside." He quickly got out, and it was just us two.

"What was that," he growled with his face as cold as a rock. "You go from nearly passing out to giving out war speeches?" I frowned when

I heard him say that; I figured Charles would be my biggest supporter. I walked closer to him, but he turned to give me only his shoulder. I turned him around so we had to look at each other.

"I had to inspire them somehow. You saw how defeated they were the second Russell's name was said," I said, motioning my hand to the people outside.

"Yeah, but you aren't exactly ready to go out there and fight some hardened soldiers. You nearly died the last time you fought!" Charles screamed at me. His voice was just as intense as before but more rattled and scared.

"That doesn't matter; they need me out there to fight. I can't just sit back and let them fight for me when I promised to protect them," I whispered to him. I grabbed his hand to try and comfort him. I knew he was bothered by my decision. He looked at our hands holding each other and pulled his away quickly.

"You nearly passed out before even hearing the news, how could you—" he started to say, but I burst over him.

"I was scared, Charles, okay. All my fears were coming true inside my head. I was freaking out and losing my mind because I was afraid, and I still am," I yelled. His stone face broke into one of concern and surprise.

"I could barely breathe, my heart wanted to jump out of my chest, I was so scared that I was going to fail, that I was all alone, and after all the love and praise this village gave me, all I did was fail them at their worst moment... but then I saw you. I saw your face and how you cared for me, and I realized I couldn't give up, that I wasn't alone. Yes, I'm still scared of failing. I know I'm not ready to challenge Russell or truly defend this village, but I know I can't just do nothing. Not when I have people who I care about counting on me." I'd never expressed myself like this, my emotions pouring out of my soul, especially to someone like Charles. I saw Charles wipe tears away from his face; I could only imagine the stress he must be in to be crying like this.

"I don't want to lose you again, Azul. I know it's been a few days since we started talking and years since we were truly close, but I feel like our bond is closer than ever and that we never truly were apart from each other. I care about you and... I love you," Charles said, his cheeks rosy and his eyes rolling streams of tears down his face.

I was taken aback by this; I had a feeling in my gut that there was something between us, but I didn't know what it was. My mind had been stuck on this village and my father; love wasn't something I thought about.

"If this is something you truly believe in, I'll be by your side no matter what," Charles whispered as he grabbed my hand. We stared into each other's eyes. Butterflies flew up in my stomach. My heart was beating like the hooves of a horse. I knew this was something.

"I love you too," I whispered as I kissed Charles, closing my eyes and putting my hands on his warm, blushing cheeks. I didn't know if he would like it, I didn't even know if I'd like it, but something in me told me it was right. For what was supposed to be a quick kiss, time seemingly stopped as our lips touched, neither of us not wanting the moment to end. I could feel his hands moving to my neck and to my back, pulling me to him, like I was his to have and he was mine. I could taste the sweat from his soft tender lips; I could feel the passion from them, each kiss more powerful than the next. It was the only thing I could feel; it was as if we seemingly left the armory and found ourselves floating through time and space. My legs felt like they were about to give out, my heart beating a thousand times a second. It was a feeling I'd never had before, and it was a feeling I wanted forever; we were the only people in the world for that moment.

I didn't want it to end, but Charles stopped. We stared at each other, faces red with our nervousness on full display. I nearly fell from how weak my legs felt, and we were both panting from the experience. We started to chuckle a little bit as we gave each other a bit of space.

"Well, I'm glad you made the first move; I don't think I would've been able to do that," he muttered. I gave him a little chuckle for it.

"Well, I just felt something in me saying to go for it," I replied. We stood there for a few seconds, not sure what else could be said or done.

"We need to get ready, Charles," I said to him, breaking the silence.

He looked a bit flustered by that, almost like he completely forgot that we were about to fight tonight.

"Yeah, you're right. I should get ready," he stuttered out of his mouth, scratching his head. As he walked out of the room, he came back and said to me in a more concerned voice, "Please be careful out there."

"I will," I said, shaking my head with a smile.

CHAPTER 6

The day went by in a chaotic storm, each man and woman tried to find some way to defend the town. Enzo ran out of bows, arrows, and blades, so hammers and the tools he used to make his armor were given as well. Most of them didn't have any protection, but that didn't stop them. As the day came to its end, I stationed myself on the balcony of Louis's tower, which overlooked the entire town.

As the minutes turned to hours and the moon rose above us like a guardian angel, the town went quiet like a mouse, each light burnt out so Russell wouldn't know where we were. I looked up at the sky to see the moon, and my, what a beautiful view it was. It looked so massive from where I was that I thought it was just a few miles away. The stars in the sky were like sparks from a fire. It felt like I was gazing at the stars for a year until cracks from tree branches in the forest returned my focus to the ground. It was them; it had to be them. I lit a torch and placed it to the side so the town knew they were here. I grabbed my bow and arrow and locked it in as I waited to see one of them walk out. They started to slither out of the darkness, but they didn't look like a force to be reckoned with. Their armor looked ill-fitting, and the usual misty steel Louis's men wore was replaced with shallow gray chainmail that was only on their chest. The rest of their bodies were covered with a thin layer of brown leather armor with thick wooden helmets to protect themselves. Their strength was crippled when Louis died, as they lost their access to Enzo's armory and their usual armor, forced to rely on scraps. Their misfortune was amusing enough to place a small smirk on my face. Anyone who had decent armor and weaponry probably went off on their own; there was no reason to stay loyal to a dead man.

I placed my bow down, grabbed the torch, and placed it next to my face, an attempt to draw their attention away from the town.

"State your business here," I yelled at the men.

They looked at each other in a confused mess; I presumed none of them expected anyone to confront them, especially not a woman. I looked around, trying to find Russell, but I couldn't find the bastard out of the horde. It was only till I heard his gruff voice laughing that I saw him, riding in with a black stallion, armored to the teeth, coming from behind his men.

"You know damn well what I'm here for. I'm here to take by *my* town," he snarled with a sadistic smile on his chubby face.

I'd only seen Russell twice in my life, but he looked the same as the last time I saw him. From what I'd heard from Enzo, he rarely left the tower or his home as he preferred to do nothing and only act in dire situations. The few teeth he had still in his mouth were yellow and looked worn down. His fat face had massive cheeks that made his brown beard even bigger than it already was and his hair was just like Louis's—a greasy, long, black mess. His armor was a lot nicer than his soldiers', a full black steel set with a massive great sword on his back and a massive steel helmet in his right arm. If you only went off his armor, he'd be a frightening sight to see, but alas, I knew he was a coward, just like Louis. I gave him a small smirk and shook my head in disgust back toward him.

"This isn't your town or Louis's, it's ours now. While you were off cowering in your home, we took it back. You and your friends aren't welcome here. Now get the hell out of here and never return!" I barked at the men below me as I set another torch on fire. They looked at each other; I wasn't sure why until some of the men let out stifled laughter. Eventually they all started to laugh. Russell was laughing so hard, he nearly choked due to the lack of air entering his body.

"Listen here, girl," he coughed out, still trying to get his breath back. "We're not intimidated by you. You're just one girl who got lucky against Louis. If anything, I should thank you for killing that slob and giving me this opening. If I was there, you'd be in the dirt, along with your old man. But alas, I had an important meeting to take care of across the river." He spoke with a sense of entitlement, like this town was created just for him to rule.

"Important business to take care of? You mean you were looking for a new way to kiss Louis's ass?" I sneered. I heard some snickers from his crew, immediately turning into silence the moment he glared at them.

"You find this all amusing? You think this little town filled with peasants is better off with you calling the shots? If it's not me you submit to, then someone else worse than me or Louis will come and force you all to obey him, and trust me, not even your luck will save you from that!" Russell yelled at the top of his lungs, clearly sending a message to the rest of the town, trying to get them to switch sides.

That statement ran in my head like a loop. There was an extremely high chance that someone else would come and try to take over, and chances are they'd be worse than what we had before. But would it be better if we lived under his protection? He couldn't even take control from Louis, how could he protect us from that threat if it came? I stood there, frozen in hesitation, weighing my options.

"This is your one chance, girl. I will spare your life since your insubordination provided me a chance to take over. I would've had to either kill Louis or wait for his fat ass to die, but you have given me an opportunity, so here's your gift. If you swear your undying loyalty to me, you and these peasants will not be harmed. If you decline it, I'll gut you like a fish. So, what's it going to be?" The demand told me all I needed to know about Russell. He didn't give a damn about any of us. To him, this was a power play, and I wouldn't let him make it on my behalf. Just as I was about to reject his offer, an idea popped up in my head.

"How about this, I come down there, and we fight, one on one. Whoever wins, rules," I coldly replied to his offer. He glanced around at his men, a look of confusion on his face, even pointing at himself as if I didn't mean to say it. He burst into more laughter, going as far as nearly falling off his horse.

"You want to fight me? You think you have the skills to beat me, no tricks, no luck, one on one?" he hollered at me. I tried to keep my cool, but his insults were getting to me a bit. "Oh girl, you must really think highly of yourself to think you have a chance."

I closed my eyes and took a deep breath, exhaling it from my nose. Then I took a deeper one. I tried to find that peace. One more deep breath, and I could feel the energy course through me. At that point, I leaped off the balcony and flipped right in from of the men, torch still in my hand. The men glared at me like I was a freak. The jump was about thirty feet, yet I suffered no injuries. I felt no pain, no stiffness, nothing; it was like I was a leaf falling from a tree, gracefully dancing in the air. I tossed the torch and took my sword out and, with two hands, pointed it right at Russell.

"I know I can." I scowled at him, glaring right into his soul. I didn't know if I could maintain control like I did on that jump, but at least no one besides me would have to die. This was my fight, my challenge, my responsibility, not the village's.

"Very well," he said as he slowly got off his horse. "Then you have a deal. I hope they already have a pair of graves for you and your father," he uttered, placing his helmet on, giving me one last smirk.

He got off his black beast and took out a great sword. The men stayed behind him, perhaps to make sure I didn't escape or to protect his flank just in case. I shifted only toward Russell. He was about the same size as Louis, but his sword was significantly bigger. That was good for me; it'd take more time for him to manage it. I had to stay away from him, use my speed to pick him off, chop him down. The last thing I wanted was to get into a sword fight with him, or a brawl. I took a deep breath and tried to channel my gifts again; I didn't need complete access to it, just enough to keep distance and fight.

He charged right at me as I tried to breathe, pointing his blade right at my heart. I rolled to the side, dodging the deadly blow, only to see him whip the blade up and prepare to swing down. His long wind-up gave me the time roll once again, this time getting to my feet as he slammed his blade where I stood.

"To be honest, I'm glad you didn't choose the smart route. I'm going to enjoy hurting you, and when you're dead, these gutless peasants will beg to be under my boot," he howled at me. He tried to charge again. This time when I rolled, I used my sword to take a swipe at his leg, cutting at his calf. It wasn't a deep cut, but it'd slow him down and cause some pain. His shriek let me know it did more than that as I turned to see he was on one knee with blood pouring out of his armor.

"You dumb bitch," he shrieked out. I took this chance and rushed him. I tried to find that inner peace, but I couldn't feel anything; I couldn't unleash it. I didn't know why, but it wasn't the time to worry about it. He lifted his blade up to pierce into my chest again, but I stepped to the side and punched him underneath his helmet, right at his chin.

It felt like my hand cracked from hitting his iron face with such force, dragging me to the ground as I lost balance. Meanwhile, Russell was on the ground, holding his face and hollering in pain. Despite the pain my hand felt, I was able to get up and drag myself to Russell, sword ready to pierce right through his skull. Just as I got it up, he quickly grabbed my leg and pulled me down, making me lose grip of my sword.

He instantly jumped on top of me, punching me right in my face. I heard a crack in my chin and nose. It was worse than what Louis or Roger did; warm blood rushed through my mouth, my nose, and from where he hit me. He smacked me on the other side, another crack rang my ears. I spat out the blood due to the force of the blow; I was gasping for air as he closed his hands around my throat. I scraped to get free, but he tightened his grip with each second.

"Not so cocky now, are you?" he barked at me. I was trapped, but something in me told me to be calm. I closed my eyes and focused only on my soul. I tried to remove everything from my mind: the warm blood covering my nose and mouth, the shattered chin, my throat being squeezed as my body got crushed. My world became dark, and for a split second, I felt the energy push through my veins, and my power came through. At that moment, I bashed my hands into his head and broke his grip. As soon as he moved his hands to his ears, I placed my hands together and smacked him in the chest, forcing him off me. I came back to reality, spitting out blood and dragging myself away from that freak. I could hear from his short breaths and screams that Russell was in a bad way too. Just as I got up, I immediately fell back down onto my knees; the pain was so great, I couldn't stomach it. *Toughen up, Azul, he's nearly dead,* I told myself. I buried my pain, grabbed my sword, and forced myself to stand. I turned to see Russell had finally gotten up too, using his sword for support. His mouth and beard were covered in blood, his helmet was removed, and his eyes were filled with anger. I guess he wasn't expecting all this from a *little bitch.*

"I won't... let this town fall into the hands of men... who only care about themselves and not... the well-being of their citizens... We will never bow to you," I fearlessly proclaimed to Russell, blood spewing from my mouth. I was nearly about to collapse from exhaustion, but I stared right into his soul as I said it.

He finally got up and lifted his blade, his face scowling at me, ready for one more charge. I closed my eyes and went back to my soul. I buried all my thoughts, all my concerns. I needed one more moment, one more clash. I buried my fears, my pain, and I focused solely on my breath, my short, ragged breath. The power coursed through me slowly, like how water slowly slips from a leaf after rain comes. I knew Russell was charging, I could feel his rumbling steps, but I wanted as much as I could muster before I swung. It built within me, and as soon as I opened my eyes, Russell's mammoth blade was seconds away from striking me down. I took my blade and placed all my strength into it as I clashed with his. The force was so powerful, I shattered his great sword and he was pushed back to his men. I stood strong, yet my jaw had seemingly dropped to the earth, not just due to my chin being smashed but from shock. I only had a few seconds of control, yet I created enough force to completely shatter his weapon and push him aside like the wind pushes around leaves.

After a few seconds, Russell finally realized what happened as he looked around, noticing where he was and the remnants of his sword.

His face was one of panic and fear. I could tell his chest was jumping as I could hear his breath from here.

"It's not possible, it's not.... Men, charge her now, kill her and kill anyone that refuses to obey my rule," he screamed out, turning to his lackeys like a child, frantically trying to put distance between us. It took a second for the men and me to realize what Russell demanded; I shook my head to make sure I heard him right.

"We had a deal!" I screamed at him. He simply ignored what I said, continuing to demand his men to fight as he crawled away. They slowly walked toward me, swords out and ready to fight. I knew they were ready to kill me, but I had my original plan to fall on.

"Fire at will," I screamed out. The second I yelled that, I ducked, and an arrow pierced right through the head of one of Russell's soldiers. I didn't see exactly what was happening in the beginning of our onslaught, though I could hear the arrows flying around. We had men stationed beneath and above the rooftop of the tower, along with my backside. The arrows flew through the air, piercing their bodies and dropping them like flies as their screams deafened my ears. Anyone that wasn't firing arrows was protecting the village with their pitchforks, swords, and the occasional knife. I figured the smartest play would be for us to take advantage of their lack of information and swarm them in their surprise, yet this plus the fight went better than I hoped for.

As I turned my head, I saw some of the raiders turn their tails and run to the forest. I wasn't too concerned about them, Russell was the one who couldn't escape. If he ran, he would come back again with a new strategy. After a few seconds of looking, I saw that Russell was lying on the ground dead with his back pierced with at least five arrows. It only took a few minutes, but after it was finished, most of his men were either dead or had fled, especially after seeing their leader dead.

"Enough!" I howled at the top of my lungs toward my force while raising my hand to signal them to stop. There was no point in firing at those scared men. Russell was dead, and they saw what we did to defend our home. As the last of them scurried away, I heard the roar of cries and cheers behind me as the townsfolk celebrated our victory.

A wave of emotions hit me as they fled, and I joined my people in the celebration. The pain in my body passed by like sweetness in the mouth. All the fear that had paralyzed my body was gone, washed away like how the rain cleansed the earth. I felt like I was reborn with this victory.

As I turned around, the crowd reacted like they'd just seen the face of God. I'd never seen them act like this as I barely heard my own thoughts from the cheers. The yells were at times incoherent, as they ranged from "our savior" and "all praise Azul" to other random screams. From the lack of injuries to them and how excited they were, I knew I did a good job leading us to victory. No, *we* did a good job. This wasn't just me, this was all of us working together.

I had this feeling, one I rarely felt, a sense of glee and joy. There was a massive smile on my face as the village turned into a joyful mob. I felt pride and excitement pumping through my heart as they came to congratulate me, each of them providing me with hugs and praise. At the end of the crowd, I saw Charles, covered head to toe in brown leather straps, smiling at me with a look of pure happiness. I leaped at him, hugging him so tightly that I felt like I might've snapped one of his bones. We giggled for a bit from the hug as I stared into his dirt brown eyes, and he stared into mine. We didn't speak, we didn't move, we just stood there, each staring into the other's soul.

"Thank you for helping me find my courage," I said to him as I rested my head on top of his chest.

"I didn't do anything," Charles chuckled. "It was within you the whole time, you just had to take it out."

I closed my eyes and pressed my lips onto his. Though the pain in my mouth stung and there was a bit of blood still there, I didn't care. The crowd disappeared around us as if we were back in that armory by ourselves. I felt his soft hands being placed on the back of my neck as we continued to lock our lips together. I felt his heart beating with intensity in my chest; I imagined he felt my heart racing too. The butterflies in my stomach once again flew as my body was flushed with pure joy and happiness. My legs started to fall apart again, yet I didn't care. Nothing else mattered in that moment—the town was saved, and I was with the man I loved. I pulled off from Charles, and we giggled a little bit as we stared at our flustered faces. There was nothing to say; our eyes said it all as we rejoined the rest of the town in our celebration.

As the night continued, I found myself back in my house next to my father. Pierre sat with him while the battle raged on, but he left once I arrived. He had a big smile on his face when he saw me, knowing what happened, and we hugged as he left. I didn't really do much beyond sitting next to my father, besides eating the night away. I just sat there and made sure my father was okay. As I started to doze off, I heard my father whisper my name, which was more than enough to wake me up.

"Father?" I yelped, shaking my head to fight off my sleep. He was still asleep but slightly conscious, enough to recognize me.

"I heard... you won the battle... that you led us to victory... I'm so proud of you, Azul," he whispered with a short, raspy breath. My heart felt like it had floated toward heaven, with my face trying to stay stoic, but the tears started to build up. I wiped them away as I composed myself. My lungs were short of breath, but I was still able to speak.

"I love you so much, Father," I said as I kissed his hand and then his head. His breathing went from short and raspy to long and deep, telling me he had gone back to a deep slumber. I decided to follow his lead, heading to my bed, and for the first time in a long time sleeping with joy rather than sadness.

CHAPTER 7

Life in the village had fallen into a peaceful slumber since Russell's failed invasion five days ago. We stripped the bodies of their lackluster armor and weapons before we buried them, along with anything that was worthwhile from them. There was a bit of concern of retaliation, but once we realized it wasn't going to come, the mood became more relaxed and cheerful. People were more willing to talk to each other besides what they had to sell or what they wanted to buy. There was discussion of an actual church being built, an idea that many thought was impossible with Louis around. I had such overwhelming conviction that everyone gave up on God and their faith, yet they proved otherwise. Some held on, even in the shadows, to their faith. Some even thought about establishing a trade network with nearby towns and attempting to grow and improve the village. For years, survival was our only focus, but now we had a chance to make our lives better.

My life also had many positives going for me, especially since I was seeing Charles. I started going to the village more often and interacting with them. Even if it was as small as me shopping for food, it felt nice to have a conversation with my neighbors that wasn't filled with gloom and despair. Most of my time was spent trying to train and trying to control my powers with some proof of my growth. I could call on my powers a lot easier, reaching that inner peace rather quickly. Once I got it, I was able to control it for about a minute, regardless of how much I charged it. It also hadn't deteriorated my body either, I guessed since I was in control and I only used it in short doses. Yet my arm still had that dark scar on it, like the plague lingering within me as a reminder of what could happen. Whenever I was out of my armor and it was exposed, I'd wrap it up with bandages to hide it from prying eyes. I spent my nights away from everything as I stood on watch from the tower's balcony, making sure no threats would attack. As much as I enjoyed this new sense of camaraderie with the people of the village, I cherished those moments alone in the tower, alone to think of how I could improve and what I could do for my people.

My father had been doing well as of late, besides his stomach hurting when he would occasionally wake up, but he spent most of his time resting. I was concerned that he spent so much time asleep, but I knew his body was still recovering; it wouldn't be right for me to make him suffer just to cool my unwanted fears. Whenever he woke up, I made sure he had fresh food and water ready for him to drink and eat.

Though we were together, I didn't spend all my time with Charles. He had other responsibilities to tend to, like his father's farm. After my father got sick, his father died soon after, and though his mother took care of what she could, the burden to provide for them fell solely on his shoulders. We relished our time together, talking about what was going on in our lives. These tiny moments never filled our thirst for each other, despite knowing what we were responsible for, a part of me loved the thought of running away with him. We didn't need much, as I could hunt and he could farm, and the thought of living my days with the one I loved, it was a nice dream. Yet that's all it was, a dream, one we couldn't live out. After all, I promised these people I'd protect them, not to mention we had our family here. We could never abandon them, especially with everything going up for us. I supposed it was just my lovesick heart speaking for me.

Those five days felt like a blur when I woke up today, like they passed by within the snap of a finger and then suddenly, I was brought here. I went to check in on my father, and he was just like he was last night, sound asleep, though it appeared he didn't touch his food. I replaced it with a fresh plate of fruits and bread and headed out to the village to get some new supplies.

The village had the same joyful spirit as before with the market as full as I had ever seen it. I recognized most of the people there, but I didn't really know that much about them. As I walked across the market, many came up to me, asking how I was doing and trying to strike up a conversation with me. This became routine for me after Russell's failed invasion; I was liked after I took the claim as protector, but I became beloved after we defeated Russell. I tried to answer all their questions, but I felt a bit uncomfortable with how they swarmed me. I knew they didn't mean harm, that they were simply happy to see their *savior*, but it still felt weird having all these eyes on me. I felt like I was a piece of meat and they were rabid dogs. As I got through the crowd, I saw an old man staring at me from his window, his cold and bitter black eyes shooting daggers at me. I stared back at him; it was the same man who glared at me before the fight with Russell, but he refused to back down, regardless of how awkward it was. I felt a sense of unease with him, why did he disapprove of me so? Had I not saved him twice? He walked away from his window, but I marched to his house, refusing to let it slide as I slammed my fist on his door. I felt the eyes of those behind me as their whispers reached my ears, but I didn't care. My mind was attached solely to the old man. He took his time to open the door, and once he let it creak open slowly, he started to walk away in his house, his back turned to me. As I entered his home, I closed the door immediately, letting this conversation be private.

"What do you want, girl?" he growled at me, his back still facing me as he walked towards the sole chair in his room, clearly not wanting to waste time with me. As he sat, I felt this radiation of tension coming from him, and fear. Did he fear that I was there to kill him?

"Is there an issue between us, sir?" I said in a calm yet aggressive tone, my teeth clenched and my fist closed with fury. I refused to play nice with him as he made it clear he wasn't. He chuckled a bit as he went to sip his blackened drink.

"What isn't the issue between us?" he said rhetorically, glaring at me. His face was wrapped with cuts and leather-like skin. Misery stamped his forehead below his receding hairline.

"I don't know what I did to offend you, but—" I started to speak before he cut me off.

"And that's your problem, girl, you act but never think. You killed Lord Louis without thinking about the cost. You openly proclaimed this town free and killed Lord Russell without heeding his words. You are just a dumb child who pretends to be a liberator, but you're just burying this town more and more," he said with anger and passion in his voice, pointing at me, with each jab more aggressive than the last. His words cut through me like a knife through wax, mainly because they rang true. Each of my actions was reactionary; I rarely thought out a plan but rather went off my instincts. But those instincts saved this town, saved these people from the evil men who ruled this town, those men that he seemed fond of.

"You're right, I do act without thinking. And you're right, I killed Louis and Russell without a second thought. And I'd do it all over again if it meant allowing me and this town to live in peace and not have to worry about some bastard torturing and harassing us over every piece of land and food we own. So, if you have a problem with me, I hope you get over it because I'm not leaving, nor am I going to back off," I said to him with confidence and pride in my voice, standing right on top of him, glaring down at him like he was an ant on my boot.

He returned my glare, but it wasn't filled with hate, rather it was a look of condescension. "Listen, girl, I won't act like you're not a good person, but being good isn't enough. Not when the strong rule over the good...." he replied. I wasn't going to listen to his lecture over what was necessary to survive in this world.

"You're right once again. I try to be a good person, but I'm not some weak child who doesn't have the stomach to take action. I'll do whatever it takes to defend this town and those I love," I roared as I stomped out of his home.

The crowd surrounding his home had grown since I entered; they probably wanted to see what would come of the situation. Without a single thought or word to them, I pushed my way through the crowd, got onto my horse, and rode back home, ignoring their cheers and pleas.

During the ride back, my mind kept going back to what he told me, no matter how often I tried to push it aside, it kept returning. It was as if his words were ghosts, and they provided a haunting melody in the back of my mind. *Am I doing what's right? Sure, Russell and Louis were pigs, but pigs that could've been keeping back a worse vandal from taking over and tormenting us. Perhaps they were a part of a larger society, like the knights who were loyal to their kings. According to Pierre, people like me and my father would've been working the field for our liege lord who'd be serving the king who lives hundreds of miles away in his castle. Perhaps it's better to deal with the devil you know rather than the devil you don't.* I shook my head in disgust. *No,* I thought to myself. *If that's the case, we would've known something about them or at least seen their men once. Could they have been working with someone? Sure, but whoever that is, I can surely handle them, right?* A trickle of doubt began to spread in my mind. *I can, right?* Luck got me through my first two tests. Sure, I defeated Russell on my own, but even then, I struggled against him. I ran my hand down my face in exhaustion, the last thing I wanted was to have a philosophical debate over what that old man said, yet here I was, reminiscing over my choices and wondering if what I was doing was truly right.

I entered my house to the usual sound of silence, yet there was a quiet, ominous moan coming from my father's room. I cautiously walked over there, the sound growing more death-curdling, and as I opened the door, my heart dropped like a boulder in the ocean. His cup of water was knocked over, and I saw a dark shade of blood covering my father's sheets. His moans sounded like a cry of death. I sprinted to his side as my eyes ran his body down, looking for what was causing him harm. I removed the sheets and saw a massive bruise on his stomach and next to his ribs.

I lightly touched his neck, trying to feel his pulse, but it was so light, it practically didn't exist. I got up, tears building up in my eyes, to run outside and cry for help, but in an instinctual moment, he grabbed my hand. His grip was as tight as his faith to Allah. Even in this weakened state, he was able to get my attention, he *clearly* wanted me to stay with him in these last moments of his life. I gripped his hands and looked into his pale, wrinkly face.

"A... zul," he said weakly, falling in and out of this world. I tried to be strong and hold back my sorrow in front of him. Despite this, a few tears slipped down my face. I wasn't ready for this, I knew there was a chance he wouldn't make it, but I thought he would get past this. He always found a way to get past his challenges.

"I... must... confess... my lies... to you," he spat out of his mouth, coughing and moaning as he spoke. His eyes, weak and bloodshot, were stuck on me. Regardless of where his mind was, he stared right at me.

"What do you mean confess, Father?" I stuttered to him. It felt like my body was shutting down, my heart was being squeezed to a pulp, my throat could barely get air in and out as I choked on my own words, gasping for any relief.

"I... swore to your mother... that I'd protect you. I swore to always... protect you," he uttered feebly. I tried my best to follow where he was going, what he meant with his words, but my mind could barely focus on it. All I could think about was why would Allah, God, any of these *divine beings,* take this man from me. It wasn't right, nor fair. Why not take me? Why take this man? I could feel myself start to slip back to how I felt back in the village when I learned Russell was approaching.

"I... am not... your father," he whispered to me.

Right there, time stopped right when he drew those words out of his mouth. My mind, my ears, my eyes, my body, they cut off the rest of the world. No noise came to my ears besides his faint breath, trying to stay alive, and my own heart that pounded like a blacksmith smashing a hammer onto hot steel. The world went black as I could only see his pale, beaten face. It was just us two in this blacked void of a world to me.

"What are you talking about, you're not my father?" I whined as I wrangled the tears in my eyes, holding back the remainder of them, trying to keep myself together.

"Your mother... did die bringing you in... but I was not... your father," he replied softly.

"Why didn't you tell me?" I spat out of my lips. I couldn't understand why he wouldn't tell me this, why he would lie about this for my entire life.

"I felt... it was the best... way to protect you. I knew... your mother was in danger... and she made... me promise... to protect you..." he said as he violently coughed out blood. I tried to grab him some water for him to drink, but he held onto me, not letting me out of his sight. He knew, he knew this was it, that he wouldn't see another day, and in the back of my mind, I knew too. He wanted to see me off one last time, before he would face his eternal rest.

"I need... you to know... before I go... that even though you aren't my daughter... I will always love you... and you are forever my little girl..." he whispered as he fell back to his bed.

His grip loosened as his last faint breath escaped his body. He was gone, and I was devastated. I screamed for him to come back, for someone to come and help, but I knew, I knew he was gone. My body collapsed, my eyes poured tears like a storm pouring down rain, my throat rang with screams of pain and misery. Through my glittery, tearful eyes, I saw that his face had a small smile on it, that even in his final moments, he mustered up the will to embrace death with a smile.

CHAPTER 8

A week had passed since my fath... since *Adam* died, and a cloud of dread and misery followed me, suffocating my heart and polluting my mind with pain and despair. Whenever I found myself walking through the village, my pale, sickly body told them all I still carried that pain. I hadn't spent a moment training or talking to anyone, regardless of the kind words they said to me. They passed by like wind blowing by my face. I tuned everything and everyone out. Charles's hug, the words from Pierre once he learned what happened, nothing anyone could say mattered. There was no massive funeral or a memorial, I gave him a traditional Islamic burial, or as much of one as I could do. I washed his broken body, wrapped him in our best cloth, and placed him in his grave. There were no witnesses, no one to cry for him besides my dried-out tears, no duas except for my pitiful recital of an old prayer my father taught me: "*Verily we belong to Allah, and truly to Him shall we return. Ya Allah, forgive him of his sins and let him enter Jannah.*" Despite the lie I lived, this man did all he could to raise and protect me, the least I could do was give him a proper Islamic burial. I didn't want anyone else there; I didn't want their fake love, their pitiful attempts to console me. I didn't go back to my house after he was buried, I couldn't do that. All I saw in that empty husk of a building were my failures and the scars that covered my heart.

I dragged myself to the balcony of the broken tower; each step felt like I'd walked a mile. I spent all my time up there, contemplating this cruel joke of a life. I found little solace in the wine I swallowed, but it dulled the misery in my heart. I knew it was *haram,* but that mattered little to me. My *faith,* my *beliefs*, *everything*, it all meant little to me. Allah didn't save my father from the miserable existence he endured before passing away. Allah didn't save us from the Dragon as it rained fire and death upon us all, nor did the belief in law and order or divine rule when it tore through Europe. What *merciful* lord would allow this? My *own* father never wanted nor cared for me, he left me and my mother for no reason. The man who raised me, who told me I was his daughter, lied to me for my entire life. He claimed it was to protect me, but was that another lie? What *dangers* did my mother and I face after the Dragon broke the world? Who could've cared enough to hurt my mother or father that they would hunt down and kill me?

Maybe he would've told me before that beating, but he never did. Maybe he never felt it was necessary, or maybe he was scared I would've left him if I knew. The conception made the cold air sting my face just a bit more as all the warmth in my body evaporated. I loved Adam, yet would that love stayed had I known the truth? What would've kept me here had I learned the truth? Perhaps it wouldn't have mattered; he did spend so much time taking care of me, why should I care that he wasn't my true father? Yet a part of me, a tiny crevice in my stomach, believed that there was a bit of truth to that sentiment, that I would toss it all away and leave them all. A tiny part of my heart felt at one point he should've died sooner so he wouldn't suffer. I didn't care for the people here other than Charles and Pierre. I certainly didn't care about the village since it wasn't my true home. Adam was my only anchor here. Perhaps he felt that if I knew, the one thing that kept him alive would've left, and if I left, he would've been dead within a week. Sure, Pierre could've helped, but there was no guarantee they could make it on their own after Adam suffered his injury. I took out and looked at the misbaha Adam left for me, all the while, his last words ringing through my head.

"Even though you aren't my daughter... I will always love you... and you are forever my little girl."

They scarred my mind, haunting every second I was conscious, forcing me to question everything. Did he truly care for me? Or was I just his only path of survival? He did seem to truly care for me; he raised me by myself. He took me in as his own, and I wasn't his daughter. The woman he swore to was dead, and he kept his promise going. I felt a hot, salty tear run down my eye, and I swiped it away in anger.

"*No,*" I told myself, clutching the misbaha so hard that small drops of blood started to come out of my fist, covering the beads on it. "*Adam lied to me. He lied to me about everything, I can't forgive that.*" For all I knew, he could've lied about my mother. How could I trust his last words when the foundation of our relationship was built on lies?

At the same time, he would never carry a lie to his grave; he knew what would be facing him in the next life. He surely said this as a way to confess his sins not only to me but to Allah so when the Day of Judgment comes, he would face Allah an innocent man.

I glanced down at the village, looking over each of their little houses, a slight smile sprouting from my face as I thought about what was happening in them. From Charles sleeping, loudly with his snore, to the eardrum-piercing cries of the newborn child Isabel and her husband Joseph had, keeping the two up happily. I thought about how Pierre was most likely sitting by a beautiful fire, reading some book about the world before that demon destroyed it. It brought me a bit of happiness after such a miserable week.

My focus shifted when I heard the sound of a horse neighing in the distance. It wasn't loud, so I didn't think it came from the village, but it cracked through the silent glass surrounding us. I hadn't been focused on my responsibilities since Adam's death; I barely surveyed the area or planned for any defenses. Many of Russell's men fled after they saw me beat their leader; none of them would try to invade knowing what I was capable of doing. I stared into the dark void of the trees as I tried to locate the noise. I saw a glow coming from the forest on the south side of the village. As I started to walk down to investigate, I noticed another glow right next to it, and as the seconds passed, more glows. I grabbed my bow and arrow and pointed it right at the autumn orange lights that began to cover the forest, pointing three arrows at it, fearing for the worst.

Suddenly, a loud, powerful, sound cracked through the night, sending shivers down my spine as it rang through my ears and forced me to drop to my knees for my protection. The sound pierced through the sky over and over, drowning my thoughts out. I covered my ears, trying to find a second of peace to figure out what it could be, but as that second hit, I turned to see a wall of fire and projectiles pierce through the forest, tearing through the wooden houses like an axe to a twig branch. A large wave of armored horses poured through the western forest like a tidal wave. They didn't just come through the west, as another large force rushed through the east and the south, galloping and howling through the village.

Their faces were shrouded with black-gray steel. Even with the light coming from their torches, they looked like demons flying across the village. The only color I saw from them was the purple banner flying above them with a large orange eagle on it. I rose to my feet and set my bow up. No matter what was happening, I wouldn't die a frightened girl. I'd die standing, fighting for my people. I launched three arrows at the galloping men in the courtyard, but nothing came from them as they bounced off their armor. I was probably too rattled for my gifts to work, and there was no time for me to calm myself down. I just kept shooting them, pulling them back as strong as I could, hoping one would pierce an eye or break through, but the waves of steel and bodies pushed through the village. Within seconds, they started to overrun us. They broke through the doors of my peoples' homes, attacking anyone they saw and dragging them out. I screamed at the villagers to escape, but the shattering blasts, the horses galloping through, and the war yells, they were too loud. It felt like every second, another bang went off; each time I heard it, I felt the sky was being torn apart. Every time it hit the wooden homes, it sounded like bones were being violently and painfully broken.

I prepared more arrows to fire again, but with no warning, I dropped to the ground hard and cried out in pain. My eyes jolted around in a panic. *Who's near me, who hit me, what happened to me*? I placed my hand on my left shoulder and felt the small but deep hole through my armor, piercing my body. Along with it, a river of blood started to surge from it. I pressed my hand down on it to stem the bleeding, all the while, my body nearly shut down from the pain. A thousand thoughts rushed through my head as the violence continued below. Only one mattered at the time though: I wouldn't lie there and die. I closed my eyes and focused solely on my mind, trying with all my might to channel my powers. The bangs and screams caused me great stress, and as much as I tried, I barely mustered any strength. It was enough to bury the pain away. Nothing else mattered. So long as I had air in my lungs, I would protect this town. I pushed myself off the ground, grabbing my blade with my right hand and charging down the stairs. Two men were storming up, armed to the teeth, wearing full suits of black armor. I leaped onto the body of the first man, driving my blade into his heart, piercing his armor.

The man next to him kicked me right in my stomach, dropping me down a flight of stairs and nearly breaking my ribs. I had no time to react to the pain as he chased me down, ready to end my life. I grabbed the knife on the right side of my hip and slashed his ankle, bringing him to his knees. With all my strength, I jabbed it right into his eye as far as it could go. He screamed so loud, I thought he'd break my ears had he kept going a bit longer. I grabbed his knife and slashed his throat, which finally shut him up as his body dropped to the side of me. As I stood up, the screeching pain from my stomach and the piercing sensation I felt with each breath I took told me how bad my ribs were. I closed my eyes and tried with all my might to bury it, I couldn't think about it, nor could I think about my shoulder; I needed to focus. I pulled my sword out of the carcass and continued to stumble outside, where the fighting was. As I opened the door, it was as if the door led me not to my town but to Hell.

Knights rode down those who tried to escape their grasp. I saw my people, old and young, women and men, dragged out of their homes and tossed into the town square. I saw these animals slaughter anyone who would dare fight against them, butchering them and torching their homes after looting them. Across the yard, I saw a knight drag a villager out of his home, stomping on his chest and face. It took a second, but when I realized that villager was Charles, I snapped. I sprinted across the mayhem with no care for self-preservation. I leaped over these steel monsters, shoving aside their prying claws of hands. I couldn't let Charles die, not after all I've been through. With each step, time went slower, the screams and blasts became silent, the armored savages and their horses moved at the same pace as the clouds above. My vision became cloudy. The events surrounding me weren't my concern, only one thing mattered, only one person, one spot, had my full attention. As I sprinted, I saw the heathen above Charles take out his sword and raise it up to pierce his heart. I extended my arms, hoping that, somehow, I could stretch them out to steal his sword, that I could stop him and save Charles. Yet, as I got right to his face, to the point that I could see his brown eyes, he thrust his blade into Charles's heart. I tackled the bastard and jabbed my thumbs into his eyes, giving him just a small taste of what he did to me before I snapped his neck, but it didn't matter. No murder I committed would bring Charles back. My best friend, the love of my life, the only one I had left in this cruel world, was gone.

As I cradled his dead body, all my memories, all the moments I had with him, flushed to me. The times I would go to his father's farm as a child and play with him, enjoying a life of peace and happiness. Us walking into town without a care in the world, cracking jokes about the mundane items available to buy. The hours we spent together, enjoying our new life, a life *fate* had stolen from us. No, not fate, these *creatures*.

My heart, a shriveled instrument already on the verge of collapse, burst that second. I felt hot, wet tears pour down my face; I screamed out to the world, letting out guttural sobs onto his body, burying myself into his bloody chest. My tears and sweat spilled onto his lifeless face. I felt his blood gushing like a red river out of his body and onto my hands and knees, the dark red, salty water bled onto my own face. I closed his eyes and laid him on the ground, giving him one last kiss on his forehead, trying so desperately to wake up from this painful nightmare. I kept my head on his forehead, trying to regain my mind before I completely fell apart. My lungs were barely functioning as each breath I took was an attempt by me to catch up to my last breath.

As I lifted my head, I saw seven men with their swords and weapons pointed at me, ready to pounce like wolves on a wounded animal. I grabbed my sword, the only thought that emerged from my pain and rage was tossing myself at them, taking all my frustration out on these men. I had little care for my own life. I had lost Charles and Adam, my parents never cared enough for me to raise me themselves, why should I *push through* this life, why shouldn't I leave this cruel nightmare to join them? As I got ready to pounce, my eyes slipped to the faces of my villagers behind them. Their faces were covered in dirt and blood, petrified at all they'd lost and all they'd suffered. Pierre's face became a lighthouse to my mind, his face broke through my bloodlust, my desire to throw it all away. His eyes screamed terror, his face screamed fear, like the thought of me dying for nothing would cause his fragile heart to perish. Or worse, the sight of me losing what little sanity I had would haunt them for the rest of their life.

I couldn't abandon them, not then, not after I gave my word. I tossed my sword to the ground and placed my hands in the air. They dragged me and tossed my broken soul with the other victims, the ones I failed to protect.

Everyone who wasn't crying was too scared to talk; they had their heads facing down, frightened to give these demons any reason to kill them. There were about twenty of us huddled together as we waited for our fate to be determined. I lay on the ground, contemplating what my next action should be. No doubt they wanted us alive, otherwise they wouldn't bother keeping us here. My instincts screamed for me to flee. I could probably make it deep in the forest and lose most of these men, but what would happen to my town? I placed my head in the dirt as my failures began to mount in my head. All these people were here suffering because of my failure, Charles, Adam, they were both dead, and their blood was on my hands. That old man was right, I couldn't save anyone, not even myself. We would've been better off with Louis or even Russell as our leaders.

As the banging noises slowed down and the war cries stopped, one singular noise played through my ear. It was a high-pitched, squealing scream. I lifted my head to see a child, no older than two, bellowing out. I looked around and saw there was no one for the child, so I picked myself up and crawled to the boy, holding onto him, patting his back, and quietly shushing him.

"Don't worry, don't worry, baby. We're going to be okay," I whispered to the kid, caressing his head onto my shoulder, silently shushing him. The child's screams turned slowly to weeping noises, and inevitably even his weeping just turned to hard breathing. After a few minutes, two horses trotted over to us, both with large armored knights on them. One of the knights wore white armor that covered his entire body and a white cape right behind it. Though the armor covered his body, I could tell that without it, he was quite massive compared to the rest of us, at least the size of Louis. The man next to him wore the exact same suit with the only difference being his armor had a silver-white shade compared to the pure white the larger man had. He was more lean compared to the other one, yet not taller. His height and size mattered little as his presence alone brought forth a sense of intimidation I'd never felt before. There was this uneasy aura surrounding him, like I was a baby deer and he was a rabid wolf watching me, waiting for me to make a tiny mistake to break my neck.

"Which one of you is Azul?" the one in silver said to us in a quiet tone, almost nonchalantly. I surveyed the crowds; all their heads were down. No one would look at me or try to give me up. Despite everything, my failure, my unwillingness to care about their lives recently, they still wouldn't sell me out, but I wouldn't let anyone else get hurt. Not for my own actions. Though I was in pain and it was a struggle, I placed the child down and stood up, walking through the crowd to the front of these faceless men, and stared them down.

"I'm Azul," I stated with defiance. They shared a glance at each other, either out of confusion or curious over their next move, as if they came here and invaded with no plan afterwards. I highly doubted that was the case though; you wouldn't make this overwhelming attack if you *weren't* afraid of failure.

"You're the leader of this rebellion?" he said with a silky-smooth tone, yet rich with condescension. He quickly turned his head toward the survivors, as if someone might rise up to claim I was lying. "When I heard the reports from our men, I never imagined this 'Azul' wouldn't be some frail woman." *His men*, I didn't want to think about it, yet in the deepest recesses of my mind, I feared my mercy allowed this to happen. By letting those men escape, they brought these iron-clad monsters to destroy us. The proof was right in front of me. This town would've been better had I simply died in that forest or fighting Louis.

"Sorry I don't fit your perceived notion of a leader," I venomously snapped back to him,

"She's the one, my lord. I saw her with my own eyes kill Russell, and she sliced Louis's head off by herself." I heard someone yell behind me. I turned around to see it was that old bastard. He looked like he just came out of his house, no scars, no cuts, no blood on him. "She may not look like a killer, but she has these strange powers that give her strength beyond the limits of normal men."

"Is that so?" the knight said as he turned his attention toward me. Though his eyes were shrouded, I could feel his gaze over me, stalking my every expression and action, contemplating his next step just by my reaction alone. He twisted his head slightly toward the man in the white suit of armor, talking about me, no doubt, as I heard "could be useful" mentioned.

The smaller of the two men came down his horse and walked up to us, hands behind his back, as if he was protected from all by Allah himself.

"I am Augustus, emperor of the New Roman Empire," he coldly stated in a quiet voice. "Your town is under my domain. If you know what's best for you, you'll kneel before me and swear your allegiance toward me." I started, dumbfounded, at him, I figured he'd claim my town, but his cockiness, the hubris in his tone, like he was some blessing shining on us, infuriated me to no end.

"You ride us down, kill my people, and you expect us to kiss your boot?!" I barked at him.

"You should be grateful you're even getting this opportunity. You rebelled against my rule and killed two of my captains. If you were anyone else, your head would've been removed by this point," he retorted quickly but calmly.

"If that's the case, why is my head still attached to my body and not on a spike?" I spewed out of my mouth.

"You're worth more alive than dead," he said casually.

I stared at him. I tried to find his eyes, but the helmet wouldn't let me. I turned slightly and looked at my people, the people I swore to protect. How could I surrender their freedom to the man that slaughtered their friends and family? Yet why should I put my pride above their lives and get them hurt even more? I dropped onto my right knee, head bowing to him, my stomach queasy at the action alone, tears starting to swell up in my face. I could only imagine the pain this would've inflicted on Adam had he lived to see it.

"This town is yours; our loyalty is yours; we are... humble servants to the New Roman Empire." Those words were venomous, but I bit my tongue. I already caused so much suffering. *Just imagine he's Louis; you dealt with it for years,* I thought to myself. I kept my head down, though I knew if I looked up, I'd pounce at this bastard's throat. My words may have claimed loyalty, but my heart screamed revolt. I'd never bow to this man in true loyalty. It was a façade, a lie to protect my people. I swore to keep them safe, and I would, and when the second arose, I planned on slaying this man and freeing my people. I heard a snap, and the presence of the men diluted as I lifted my head to see them marching away, falling into file. Their weapons placed to their side, heads bowed down. I turned to see the rest of my people still looking at the ground, fearing their own fate.

"Glad to see you came to your senses, Maximus. Leave fifty men here to make sure they stay *loyal*. You," he stated with a steady tone, pointing toward the old man, who looked shocked. "Your service and loyalty to your lord has been commendable, you'll be rewarded justly." The old man looked like his heart nearly gave out from that news.

"Thank you, my lord, I live to serve you," he said, dropping to his knees and bowing to his *god*.

"The girl will join us on our trip south where we'll see what she's worth. We'll leave when the sun rises," he proclaimed to us. I couldn't believe my ears. My face clearly showed that confusion as he asked me, "Is there an issue, girl?"

"Why are you taking me south? Why not just leave me here?" I spat back to him.

"Like I said, you're worth more alive than dead. We'll see if what we've heard has any credibility to it," he retorted back.

"And if I refuse?" I questioned. I realized I was no longer on my knees; I was standing, fist clenched. Was I purposely trying to be defiant? I already surrendered; why was I fighting like this? He walked up to me, still providing a bit of space, but I could feel an overwhelming terror in my gut.

"Then we'll burn this town to the ground along with everyone here, forcing you to listen to them as they scream and beg for mercy, and when they're all dead, we'll kill you too," he coldly stated to me. Just like that, death sounded like a blissful escape. Allah had already dropped me off in Hell, and I wanted out so bad. I thought about just... but it left as quickly as it arrived. I wouldn't die; I'd survive to spite this monster. And when he least expected it, I'd rip his heart from his chest.

"Fine, as long as I have your word that my people will be safe and treated well by your men," I quietly responded.

"As long as you listen to me, no harm will come to your people. If there's one thing you can count on, it's that I always keep my word," he testified to us. He turned his head slightly to the right, looking at the men behind us. "You two will be in charge of protecting our *guest*. Make sure she doesn't escape."

Most of the men started to go back into the forest, no doubt to their camp. The few remaining started to clean up the ravaged land, taking anything worthwhile off the dead bodies. The victims started walking back to their homes, trying to deal with the destruction they had just witnessed, and their grief for it all. All the while, I just stood there, I stood and stared at my broken village, looking around at the devastation surrounding me, the bodies that lay on the ground, the burning homes. The smell of burnt flesh and death practically killed all the sense in my nose, a disgusting display of my failure. The men, one of whom was holding my sword and scabbard, clamped cold, hard steel around my hands and started to pull at it, signaling me to move. As I walked, I could see Pierre walk over to Charles's body. He turned his attention to me and nodded, a simple sign that he'd watch over the people and do all he could for them while I was gone. As we began our march to their camp, I could feel tears starting to build up in my eyes. I couldn't use my hands without them being yanked, but I wiped them away with my shoulder. I won't let them see me as a broken victim. I'd make them regret this if it was the last thing I did.

CHAPTER 9

Their camp was about two miles west of the village, deep within the forest. It was the perfect staging ground to launch their assault. The camp looked like a little village with all its tents, animals, and smoke that came from it, along with about three thousand men waltzing through the campground. There were numerous banners, each holding a different sigil on them, but all of them had a purple background and an orange tilt that surrounded it. My leather clothes did little to stop the cold, as the steel cuffs started to tear into my skin. I felt the blood dripping off my fingers, the steel going back and forth, ripping and scarring my wrists. My feet were soaked in mud, and since I barely felt them, probably my own blood too. No doubt blisters formed and popped during this *trip*. The only thing I felt in my feet was a slow, crushing pain that lingered in my toes. A pain that felt like I drove a sword right through it and kept pushing it down, slowly mushing it from side to side. As I arrived, several of the men were taking their gear off and getting ready to sleep. The potent stench of boiled liquor and human waste destroyed whatever existed of my nose. It didn't get better as after a few minutes adjusting to that stench, I got stabbed with a strong whiff of sweat, grease, and other smells I could barely describe. Though even if I knew how to describe them, I felt it was better to ignore them.

I felt a slight yet stern tug at my chain, a sign that I'd spent too much time standing in one place and I needed to move. I felt the watchful eyes of the men glaring at me like I was being brought to my execution. Their stares, in truth, didn't bother me so much as their silence; not a single word was spoken while I walked through the camp. I preferred

Louis's nonsense over this; at least I knew I was alive there, I wouldn't be executed for that. I pretended to ignore their glares, staring straight ahead, practically drilling holes into the head of my guards, but I wanted so bad to be anywhere but here. Regardless if I was dead or back at home, I'd give anything if it meant I was invisible again.

We eventually stopped at the western side of the camp, where there was a small wooden encampment with a pole right in the middle of it. I imagined this was where I'd be spending my night as they tied me up to the pole and tossed a thin blanket to keep me warm. As they tied me up, one of the men walked up to us. It took him a few moments of just staring for him to finally say what was on his mind, asking for me to dance and show off my "presents." I heard some of the men, including my guards, start to giggle a bit and make similar comments, but I wouldn't give them any satisfaction, whether it was me being hurt and sad or just angry. I simply stared off into the forest, hoping that this nightmare would end and I'd wake up back home. Once they were done, I lay on the ground with the blanket wrapped around my shivering body. I barely slept. Any time I fell into unconsciousness, the screams of my people would roar in my head and all I would see were their bodies piled up, ready to be burned down. Each time those nightmares passed through, tears ran down my eyes. Why was I here, what was I doing, sitting in that camp surrounded by these demons? What *just God* could do this to anyone? I tried to bury my thoughts and hide in the darkness of my mind so I could sleep. I knew I had a long day ahead of me, and I would need all my strength.

After what felt like hours, I finally fell into a deep slumber before the roar of a loud trumpet brought me back from the dead. I woke violently from the ground, the dirt stuck on my face and hair. Groggy, I dusted myself off and rose, only for my chains to bring me back to the pole. It came back to me like a nightmare. I saw the men running around the camp, getting themselves prepared for presumably the long march ahead of us. As I slowly got back onto my feet, I noticed my body felt a lot better and my wounds had healed up nicely. However, as I looked down, I noticed it. The black blood right next to where I slept.

It wasn't a lot, but I knew what it meant. I took off my left glove and saw that the black scar ran all the way past my wrist, covering most of my hand. It didn't hurt, but anything that looked like this couldn't be good. My powers must have been pushed to new limits to keep me alive. Though my shoulder was a bit stiff, the wound had fully healed and left only the bloody mess on my clothes and body. The blood had soaked right through the leather armor and left me with a sticky, smelly stench. The fact I could smell it so strongly and breathe with no issue told me my ribs were fine too. I noticed none of the men were that clean, so I doubted there'd be a chance for me to cleanse myself, not that I wanted to with these animals prowling around. I put the glove back on; I didn't want too many prying eyes on what I could do here.

The men *responsible* for me finally returned after a few minutes of me waiting. They removed my chains from the post and pulled me to the outskirts of the camp where the bulk of the army was lined up, besides a few stragglers. As I walked toward the back, each soldier just stared off to the front, ready to march. I recognized some of them as the men who asked me to warm their beds last night, now unfazed by my presence. As I got there, it took perhaps a minute for another trumpet to go off, this time with two quick blows, signaling to the men to start marching. Each row moved with haste yet calmly so they wouldn't tire out quickly. They all marched in rhythm with each other, so no one was out of sync. Even the two men on horseback watching me stayed on pace with them; I was the only one who struggled to stay in rhythm. Whether it was my exhaustion, my hatred of these men, or just my lack of experience, I didn't know what I was doing. I started to drift behind them, but after a yank of my chain by one of the men, I leaped back into position. It worked for a bit, only until I found myself right on the ass of the knight in front of me. It took some time, but finally, I found myself in rhythm with the rest of the men. The marching was torturous to my legs. With each step, it felt like my muscles were being torn slowly, one tiny piece at a time. After a while, they simply went numb, and I felt no pain. I couldn't stop marching; I was stuck in a loop, a slight blessing, I supposed. All I heard during this march was the footsteps of everyone.

No one spoke; there was no chatter, no songs being sung, no trumpets or drums, just the sound of boots slamming into the dried earth.

As we kept marching to what felt like my grave, I noticed one of the white-armored knights riding next to us, watching over us on horseback. He was silent, yet his glare seemed to be judgmental enough to speak for him. It was only after I passed by that he returned into formation, though he was right beside me.

"How was your sleep last night?" he asked me kindly. I recognized from the voice that it wasn't Augustus but rather his son, Maximus, I believed. Regardless, I wasn't interested in having a discussion with him. That was, until one of my *guards* smacked me in my stomach with his staff. The hit was swift yet not too painful, just enough to get my attention and obedience, I guessed. I stumbled a bit, nearly falling to my knees to catch my lost air, only able to keep myself standing through sheer will.

"Answer the prince when he speaks to you, wench," he scolded. Every fiber of my being wanted to rip his head off, but I knew that would get me and my people tossed into a shallow grave. I swallowed what little pride I had and gave the punk a rebuttal.

"I slept like a log," I said with no energy. I heard a chuckle come from the armored scoundrel. I failed to see the humor in this situation, but maybe it was because I wasn't a soulless bastard.

"I can only imagine how miserable you must've been, captured and surrounded by the men who raided your town. Forced to sleep with us..." Each word was filled with condescension as he looked down on me.

I couldn't help myself as I quickly retorted, "You have no idea." There was a bitter sting in my voice, all my hate directed toward that stupid helmet, like I was trying to crush it with my mind.

"You're right, I don't. I'll see to it that you'll have your own tent and be treated like the other men here. It's the least I can do," he said solemnly. I wasn't sure how to respond. He went out of his way to give me this kind action, something I thought none of these demons could provide. It left me stunned and speechless.

"I'll take your silence as a thank you," he said as he started to ride off. Just before he got out of earshot, those words finally came out of my mouth. He seemed to hear it since he turned back in my direction, nodded at me, and continued to ride ahead.

We marched for what felt like an eternity through the forest. Who knew how much distance we made, but it was the farthest south I'd ever been. As we finally stopped, my legs felt like they were about to pop off my hips. They felt so numb, I had to take my boots off. That's when I noticed the blood that had drenched my feet. I heard from some of the men's chatter that we'd stopped to hunt near the river, get some clean water, and make sure we were on the right path. The river was much like the one back home, blue like the sky, yet it didn't have the same strength as mine. It was smaller, but I still saw some fish swimming through it. As we took a brief rest, I sat next to the river to provide some relief for my torn, blood-soaked feet by placing them into the cool water. I sat there, blissfully ignoring the others and coming to terms with what my options were. I knew I couldn't run away, but I had to figure out what to do if I wanted to survive and get out of this mess. Sticking with this army would almost surely end poorly for me, and if I fled, there was no guarantee I could make it out of this forest alive. Even if by some miracle I did, they'd know exactly where I'd head off to, or at least where I'd want to go. I wasn't even sure where home was from here. By the time I found it, they'd probably burn my village to the ground. I couldn't risk their lives; I needed to come up with a plan to save us.

As I sat there, I felt a wooden cup touch my shoulder. I turned around to see a skinny, fair-skinned, pig-nosed boy with a patchy beard missing a mustache in front of me. He had a small smile on his face and a pair of cooked fish on sticks to go with the wooden cup in his hands.

"My apologies if I startled you, girl. I saw you were sitting here by yourself, and I wanted to offer you some food and water," he said kindly as he handed me the food. A part of me wanted to shove the fish down his rotten and yellow teeth, but he was much too kind for me to do such a thing. I took him up on his offer, chugging the long necessary water down and quickly devouring the fish.

"Thank... you," I said, confused, still tearing through the fish. "Why would you do this?" He shrugged his shoulders, like giving food to the woman who fought against his ruler was probably not an act of treason.

"Figured you'd be hungry from all that marching. I remember my first day as a part of this army. I couldn't walk right for a week," he said with a goofy smile on his face. "Oh, my apologies, I didn't introduce myself, I'm Arthur." He stuck his hand out toward me. I slowly extended my own and shook his hand, all the while staring at him and wondering what else could be motivating him.

"I didn't imagine any of you would be so kind," I said coldly as I turned toward the river and tossed the bones in the water.

"Well, that's cause you've only seen us on the battlefield," he responded. "Tough to know a man when you've seen him at his most savage." I turned my head to see he was looking around. He pointed at the two men behind us.

"Like these two beside you. Their names are Antonio and Razul. They're brothers who've been supporting their family off their earnings. Most of the men here are supporting their families with this," he said.

"Then why join it? I presume they need farmers in their towns," I responded.

"Our lord called upon us. We live under his dominion, and when he calls for our swords, we rise for him," he said. "It gives me great pleasure knowing I'm serving a higher purpose than myself."

"Oh really, and what's that higher purpose?" I quickly retorted. To which he just pointed at the flag.

"The New Roman Empire. We're fighting for a return to society, to civilization. It's our duty to reclaim what was taken from us, our duty to rebuild what was destroyed, as our lord puts it," he said, his voice proudly proclaiming his sense of pride as he ate his own fish. I stared at the flag and thought over his words, recalling a conversation I had with Pierre about the former empire.

"But Rome's been gone for more than a thousand years. Why go back to that?" I asked. His face was scrunched up a bit, like he wasn't sure why I'd bother to mention such a statement.

"Girl, when Rome was at its peak, there was no civilization that could rival it. There was no place on this planet that could compete with our realm. Emperor Augustus said it best: 'Why settle for our families' desecrated land when we can rebuild what our forefathers left for us,'" he proudly stated.

"Augustus," I said to myself with resentment and bitterness in my voice. "What type of leader is he anyway?"

The boy's face shifted from joy and pride to a stoic gaze. He sat down next to me, sweat starting to bead more on his face, taking a hard swallow of his remaining food.

"He's a great leader, harsh but fair, none of this could be possible without his commitment, his vision," he replied with some of the pride in his voice gone, left with an indifferent tone. "We'd just be a bunch of insignificant specks without his guidance."

I turned to look at the boy as he stared at the ground. His face lost a bit of color, but he also lost something else. He was antsy, his eyes darting around; his words said one thing, but his actions screamed fear. Fear of *his lord* hearing him or fear of his brethren hearing him talk poorly of their king, I wasn't sure.

"Is this what you truly believe, or is this what you've been told to believe?" I whispered. He turned his head in shock, as if this was such a foreign concept to him. "Is this the path you wished to take or one you're forced on?"

He took a second, his jaw clenched and his face hardened before he responded, swallowing, I assumed, his fears of being heard.

"It matters not what I want or believe, you're a part of the empire, girl. Our survival is dependent on our unity. Now if you'll excuse me, I must return to my compatriots," he quickly replied, rising to his feet and walking into the sea of armor-clad men.

The change in his attitude and his answer, he may not have said it, but it told me the grip Augustus had on his men. He went from joyful to crutched with fear within the moment I mentioned Augustus's name; though I must say, I could be scratching at something that didn't exist. These men owed their loyalty to Augustus as he was their lord.

Much like how peasants owed their loyalty to the nobles and kings whose land they lived on in a previous world, in a previous generation, when Dragons were just myths and men ruled by birthright. It made sense he'd want to revert back to that world, taking all the power for himself and stripping his men of it. Yet it didn't make sense why his men would listen to him.

He didn't seem to be a young man. Most likely out of his prime, they wouldn't fear what he'd do to them with his bare hands. Loyalty was hard to come by, especially in this world when you're proclaiming yourself an emperor. All that would do is place a target on his head. I'd never heard of the New Roman Empire, nor had I heard of Augustus. Even if Louis was supposedly loyal to him, he never mentioned it. That old man who sold me out knew of him, yet Pierre never talked about him. Were we loyal to him? Why would these men fight for him, serve him, fear him? Why would anyone be loyal to a man they didn't even know? My mind jumped through many different answers as to why they swore fealty to him. It could be that he provided law and order in his empire, keeping his people safe so long as they continued to fuel his army. Yet all of the kingdoms fell after the Dragon, what made Augustus any different? All signs pointed to him being just like so many other monarchs I'd heard of, taking the lands from peasants and ruling through fear and power. But that would have created a lot of tension among the people and soldiers, tensions that would unravel and lead to a civil war.

Perhaps he used religion or a common bridge to bring these people together peacefully. He could've easily wiped us out if he wanted, yet he chose to keep us alive, killing only to win the battle and nothing more. He spoke to us like he didn't want to needlessly kill, that violence was a last resort for him. That said, he chose to invade the town anyway, but was that because he knew we wouldn't surrender? Some of Russell's men probably got to him, giving him all the information necessary to destroy us. If he was truly a man of peace, a man of God, a man who used violence only when necessary, why only show such a violent, dark, ugly side of oneself? Why would he allow someone like Louis to rule and stay in the shadows? Louis wasn't any sort of Godly man, nothing like my fath...

I did it again. The thought of Adam shredded whatever was left of my heart and brought forth a flood of emotions I yearned to remove. My face became hot with pain and suffering, my eyes slowly got more wet, and my tears started to build up. I took his misbaha out and just looked at it, the craftsmanship, the design of the light brown pieces, the touch of red on the beads, probably my blood from how hard I held it. Though it was a hundred beads tied to a string, it was enough to calm me down as it reminded me of a better time. A time when my life was peaceful, a time when the only monster was Louis and I still had a father, even if it was just a lie. One where all this pain was nonexistent, where my life wasn't dangled like bait for the wolves. What I would give just to have that life again.

That sliver of peace was taken quickly after one of these steel-clad apes let out a howling noise into the air, tearing apart the silence. My heart nearly pierced out of my body, and I almost fell into the river. As I lifted my head and looked around, most of the men didn't notice my reaction or share it as they looked undeterred by the ghastly sound that was made. The men *protecting* me barely moved or looked at me; they were too focused on the cooked fish on their plates. I shook my head to regain my composure, and as it slowly came back to me, I heard the sound of iron boots tapping on the earth, lurking toward me.

"Never seen one, have you, girl?" he said to me. I turned to see it was Maximus, holding his helmet to the right side and whatever made that terrible sound to his left. It was the first time I'd seen what he looked like. His hair was golden blonde, his eyes matched the color of the dirt, his nose was short yet slightly pointed, his chin, jawline, and cheeks were very sharp and distinctive. His skin was fair, though thanks to that hot, heavy armor, his face was pink and sweaty, and there was no beard on his face to hide it. He looked young, probably around the same age as me. There were yellowish stains on his teeth, but they were all there. In fact, it didn't look like he had any scars on his face.

"Other than when your army was firing it at me and my town, no. What is it?" I said.

"It's our army now, and this is a gun," he said plainly.

"A gun?" I uttered, confused.

"Do you not know what a gun is?"

I shook my head no as his face turned to one of surprise, and after a few moments, he presented the gun to me. The first thing I noticed as I held it was the weapon felt heavy, heavier than I had anticipated. It was long, a bit longer than a usual broadsword. I could smell the rich scent of iron from the gun, but it looked to be made of some wood, maybe maple? There was a burning smell coming from it as well, but I couldn't tell what it was. At the end of the gun, there was a knife coming out, which must be for charging at someone.

"A gun is a weapon that can fire these bullets from a certain range and will pierce through armor and the body," he said as he placed the bag of bullets in my hand. "They're much more powerful than your bow and arrow and eliminate the need for close combat that a sword requires, but the blade in the front allows for you to kill someone if you were to run out of bullets." As I looked around, I noticed not everyone had a gun, like my *guards,* as they only had swords on their sides.

"If they're so powerful, why doesn't every man have one?" I asked him quietly, almost like this was some taboo topic.

"Well, they're not easy to make; most of these guns are old and might not even work that well thanks to their age," he said.

"Well, if these guns are so old and they may not even work, why not make more?" I asked him, confused.

"Yes, son, why not?" I heard from behind me. I didn't need to turn around to know it was Augustus who stood over us. I looked to see him on top of his horse, with his white suit reflecting the sunlight into my eyes, practically blinding me.

"All the equipment for it was destroyed," he said with a slight change in his voice. It wasn't massive, just a subtle switch up. His confidence wasn't all the way there in his tone, and he seemed a bit more on edge as his shoulders slowly went up from slouched to straight. I thought back to how I was with my father even before his last days on this planet, and nothing would've gotten me to this level of stress and pressure. If he could do this to his son by just asking a simple question, Arthur's reaction made more sense.

"By what?" he asked once again to his son, his hands on the helm of his sword and the leash of his horse.

"By the Dragon," I quickly stated back to him as I stared right into his helmet. He turned around and looked right at me, my eyes squinting from the light.

"Correct, when the beast set our benevolent continent on fire and destroyed our divine civilization, most of the main gun manufacturers were burnt to the ground. The powder used to fire these bullets are very flammable, which caused even more destruction as those manufacturers exploded from the heat." He calmly said to me.

"From the reports of my scouts, most people didn't die from the Dragon but from the destruction that the flames created. A large crate of gunpowder, on top of the Dragon's fire is enough to destroy an entire town; a whole manufacturer of it can burn an entire countryside to the ground. Most of these guns and gunpowder were made before the Dragon destroyed the world." During his *lesson*, he was pointing at his men and their weapons, but it felt like his eyes were on me the entire time. As if he was watching my every move, learning about me as much as he could. I did feel some of that pressure on me, but perhaps my anger toward him blinded me from the effects of that pressure.

"Well, given how big your army is, and if about half of them are walking around with guns, I imagine it's not the smartest decision to be roaming around with enough firepower to burn down an entire forest along with us," I said sarcastically. I felt an iron hand grabbing my left hand tightly. I saw it was Maximus, who stared at me like I'd committed a murder.

"Perhaps, but any leader worth his salt knows the army that's better equipped will win a battle nine times out of ten. No army, sword, or gun at hand can defeat the beast. Only a fool like that French king will try to fight it off. This army isn't designed to fight the Dragon, it's designed to fight men, and there's no point in leaving my men without the best tools available to defend themselves," he eloquently stated. My mind quickly went to the bodies of my people, my friends, to Charles. I didn't care about my pledge, I didn't care for my oath. I wouldn't sit there and allow this man to lie.

"I doubt you care about those who serve you so long as they kiss your boot," I said bluntly. In the corner of my eye, I saw Maximus's face turned practically white after that, like I had spat in the face of my executor.

"Your opinion means little to me, girl, for you see just a speck of the picture, a picture that engulfs all of western Europe and soon to be the rest of the Mediterranean. Whether you believe it or not, these men fight for me and they're under my guidance; without them, there is no New Roman Empire, an empire, last I checked, you swore fealty to," he said patiently, like he was talking to a child.

"I'm fully aware of my pledge... my lord," I uttered back to him. He nodded his head and started to ride away toward another section of the makeshift camp.

"What a ray of sunshine," I muttered to myself. Before I knew what happened, Maximus grabbed my shoulder tightly, doing all he could to restrain his anger toward me.

"You *will* not disrespect him like that again, you understand me?" he said to me, vicious and straightforward. I yanked my shoulder out of his grasp and rolled it around to get the blood flow back. I glared back at him, my anger starting to boil over. Who was he to tell me this? I didn't care if I claimed this *boy* as my prince; I wouldn't hold back my feelings to him.

"Or else what? He's going to attack my town and burn it to the ground?" I retorted sharply.

"I understand you're hurt and frustrated, but you're messing with the wrong bull, my father..." He paused for a brief moment as if what he was going to say might have serious repercussions. He took a breath and then continued in a quiet tone. "My father isn't the type of man who'll take insubordination lying down," he responded.

"Your father has captured me and took my life away, why should I show him respect?" I said bluntly. He looked slightly confused, like he wasn't sure what to say. Obviously, the answer would be that I proclaimed Augustus as my emperor but clearly my actions didn't scream loyalty to the crown. He looked around for a second, closing his eyes as he took a deep breath and looked back toward me.

"Because whether you like it or not, he controls your fate. I understand your frustration, but if you want to return home, to any resemblance of your old life, you have to play the game and survive. If you do that, there'll be no reason for him to harm you or those you pledged to protect. But if you—"

"Be a bitch, I'll die," I said, interrupting his statement.

"Disrespect him, and you'll die, along with those who live in your town," he said coldly. I knew what he said was correct, being aggressive would only lead to a shallow grave for myself. Yet a thought ran across my mind about this man.

"Why do you care what happens to me?" I asked him. He looked like a statue when I asked him that, no emotion on his face, but I presumed he was in thought.

"Tell me, did you know who ruled over you? Not Louis, but the man Louis took orders from?" he asked me.

"No, I reckon now he followed your orders, but, before, I believed he worked alone. The way he proclaimed himself a god gave me no reason to believe he had others to answer to," I quickly retorted back to him.

"Exactly, girl. You had no idea of us and who truly ruled you. Had you known the truth, you could've come and informed us of his heinous actions, and we would've taken care of him," he said with a civil tone.

"You're telling me your father would take away one of his captains just like that?" I asked, a large amount of doubt in my tone. Why would his father cater to peasants complaining about his lords? He would gain nothing by doing that, and if anything, it signaled that he wasn't strong enough to stick to his original convictions. Right? I thought about it, but I could see how it could work. He wanted to be like Rome; Rome had a Republic, which according to Pierre, allowed the citizens some power. But did this man view us as citizens or as slaves?

"Just like that. He had plenty of good lords he could've sent down to enact his rule, he just didn't have a reason to send one down. He wants this empire to be perfect, and that includes helping those who suffer from tyrants and those without the power to overwhelm their tyranny," he responded.

I was surprised to hear this. The idea that Augustus cared that much about his men being good to their people baffled me. The idea that he would give more than a glancing thought about us *peasants* was even more shocking.

"I can't believe it," I said, stunned.

"That's why I don't want to see you toss your life away, because I believe you weren't in the wrong. You didn't know of my father's rule, and you simply were defending your father when you killed that buffoon. If you knew, you would've realized there was another option available for you to take. You don't deserve to suffer for that," he said as he started to get up and walk away from me, allowing me to digest his words and leaving me with one last statement to feast on. "Please, Azul, don't do anything stupid."

CHAPTER 10

After an hour or so had passed at the camp, we started to march once again through the forest. Though I struggled to get back into rhythm, I eventually found my way. My mind throughout the journey was distracted by what happened at the camp. I thought about the reactions of Arthur and Maximus toward Augustus. It seemed like Augustus had a firm grip on his soldiers' fear and loyalty, but what was that fear based off of? What made this old man different from the rest? He seemed to be an old man, yet I wasn't sure, I hadn't seen his face. I knew Europe didn't belong to kings and their old families anymore, otherwise the French royal family wouldn't have been murdered and burned alive by the peasants in Paris. Perhaps he had enough resources to pay these men, but why not just cut his throat after they got paid or rob him right from the start? There was no reason to be loyal to someone or even fear them when you were part of a larger force. Even if they only served Augustus for his wealth, it wouldn't explain the fear his name enforced. The worst he could do was take their wealth or land away, which could spark a civil war and his death.

I clearly didn't have all the pieces to this puzzle. As much as I wanted to slit Augustus's throat and move on, all that would do was guarantee the death of my people and me. There was clearly more going on than they let on. It seemed like Maximus knew that Louis was an awful human, and yet all we needed to do was complain and Louis would've been gone? I simply didn't have enough information to do anything but wait it out. What I did know was Augustus was the key, the head of this poisonous snake, the wolf that led the pack. I needed to kill him for this empire to be destroyed. Most likely these men would have no reason to stay united if their emperor wasn't breathing anymore. The New Roman Empire would cease to exist. Maximus might be able to keep some of their loyalty, but if I knew one thing about the men who fought for Augustus, it was that they were power hungry. They'd betray each other for any scrap of land they could take.

Yet all that would do is create another power vacuum, and they'd kill whoever they could to grab whatever power they could get their hands on. There were already fifty men at my town now; what was stopping them from killing my people or enslaving them once the news of Augustus's death spread there? I could probably fight them off, but what if I couldn't? What if my gifts weren't enough? I promised my people I would protect them and keep them safe. The best way I could keep them safe was, as Maximus put it, "play the game." As much as it killed me, there was no other play I could make besides being loyal and *serving* my emperor. At least, until I get more information on how this empire operated. Once I knew how I could destroy it without leading to my people's death, I would break it like a twig.

We kept marching for what felt like days, though I knew it was only a few hours. The sun started to set, and the darkness of the night slowly encircled us, the forest becoming harder to see. As we kept moving, a small yet bright light started to form from the left side of the forest. I thought it was just a man walking with a torch, but as I got closer, that light grew in size and brightness until, eventually, we had to halt our march because of it. The light came from a cave in the forest, practically blinding us. I could hear the muttering of the men talking about it, and Maximus yelling at his father about the cave, that they needed to "investigate it." I saw Augustus peel out from the front of the army to our side, in front of the cave.

"Any volunteers to investigate the cave?" he yelled in a loud yet smooth tone, one that carried a sense of intimidation.

We all stood in silence, some looked at the ground as they avoided eye contact with him. Some of the men looked at each other, hoping one of them would step up. Their hesitation was curious to me to say the least.

I imagined they were afraid of what the light represented rather than the actual light. For all they knew, it could be a tiny Dragon, gleaming in the remaining sunlight, gathering its strength. Perhaps it could be a portal to Hell, slowly dragging the world down until it was the Day of Judgment. Regardless, these men seemed petrified of it and remained silent. I took a step forward and stared right at him.

"I'll go," I said sternly to him. He immediately turned his head around toward me, and if I could see his face, I envisioned his silence would be followed with a dumbfounded look on it.

"You volunteer?"

I nodded my head yes as quickly as he asked me. I heard some laughter from the back, but I didn't give it any focus. He hopped off his horse and walked to me, each step silencing those around me until we were face-to-face. "Yesterday you were a rebel against my rule, what's with the change of heart?"

"My emperor requested a volunteer, am I not honor-bound to serve you... my lord?" I said to him with a subordinated tone, no humor, no sarcasm, no emotion.

"That would imply you took your oath seriously," he quickly retorted back to me.

"Emperor Augustus, I am nothing if not honest. I would never claim anything if I plan on not following through with it," I stated back to him with as much speed as he did to me. I heard a little chuckle come from his iron body, like he could supposedly see through my statements.

"I have no doubt you're honest and willing to take your oaths seriously, but for me? Someone a few hours ago you claimed doesn't care about those who serve me? I highly doubt that."

"Emperor Augustus, I made a pledge to my people to protect them, and I know the only way I can do that is serving you," I said to my *king*. I was focused on survival; I was focused on making it out of this situation alive. I was focused on ripping his heart out and feeding it to himself. Only way to do that was to earn his trust, to learn what made his empire work and use that to break it. He thought about the decision and nodded his head at Razul, who cut my rope and shoved me to Augustus.

"You'll investigate the cave and report back what you found there. We've heard reports that bright lights like this are a nursing ground for the Dragon and it's attracted to it," he said to me. Made sense why the men wanted no part to do with this; they feared the Dragon coming to annihilate them. I shook my head and started to walk toward the cave.

"And girl," he said to me. I turned around to him and his men. "If you try to run, we'll track you down and kill you," he said quietly yet firmly. I shook my head nervously.

The cave was about thirty yards away from the path we were traveling on, and it wasn't that big. It was about nine feet tall and wide but looked man-made with a steep decline at the end. As I got inside the rocky crevice, I could barely see with the light flashing. Even as I covered my eyes and squinted, all I could truly see was the light. With each step, I felt the cave closing in on me more and more, swallowing me alive. I had to bend my knees and back just to pass through it. I found myself on my hands and knees, scraping through the dirt. Each step, the light grew brighter; each step, the cave felt hotter, like I was facing the full weight of the sun in the middle of summer. Sweat poured down my face as I crawled. I had to stare at the ground just to avoid the light blinding me. Eventually, I reached my limit. I could no longer squeeze my way through the cave. I was practically stuck; my knees, hands, and elbows were dripping in blood. I reached out toward the bright light and tried to touch whatever was there. I felt the heat of a great fire radiating from it, but it didn't burn my skin as I got closer to it.

As I touched whatever the heat was coming from, I felt a little flower at the end of my hand. I grabbed the stem of it, and as I pulled, the light disappeared almost immediately. The cave around me vanished; the blood on my body was gone, along with the scars that covered it. I was in that same blue dress as before. I looked around and saw there was nothing around me, just a pitch-black world that engulfed me. I looked at my hand and saw the flower was gone, but as I looked up, I saw a man on his knees, bloody and wounded, staring off into the distance, blade by his side and a blue rose in his hand. His skin was dark brown, and he wore thin steel armor around his legs and arms, but I could see his chest piece was tossed away, along with his helmet. He wore a dirty white top, covered in sweat, blood, and dirt. He had thick black hair covered in sand, and there were bits of blood in his thick beard. Sand started to fill the ground around me, and my sight became more clear. I could see the clear blue sky surrounding him, the desert practically eating his knees and feet. His eyes were the same radiant blue as my own. I heard a bit of a murmur coming from him; it was low and weak, but it sounded like Arabic. He took the flower and forced it down his throat. It took a few seconds, but he swallowed it. He then grabbed the blade and closed his eyes, repeating the same thing over and over.

Tears running down his face, he whispered to himself, "Lā 'Ilāha 'Illā Allah, Muḥammadun Rasūl Allah." *There is no God but Allah and Muhammad is the messenger of God.* He took a deep breath and jabbed the blade into his gut.

After a brief yelp, he whispered one line.

"Ya Allah eaqib aladhin zalamuni wahfazhum..." *Ya Allah, punish those who wronged me and protect...* Then he drowned into the desert, the ground seemingly eating him whole. The dirt started to shake, the sand under my feet grew hotter. The small clouds above me diluted till there was only the blue sky and the boiling sun, fueling the heat even more. The spot where the man was buried shook furiously, raging until the brown sand started to turn black, but then I realized that the black sand wasn't sand. The wings started to pierce through the sky, the tail slowly rose over the desert hills, and the beast's head emerged right where the body dropped, its blue eyes staring directly at me. It roared to the sky, firing its molten flames into the atmosphere, driving the heat to apocalyptic levels. The beast slowly lowers its face toward me, walking toward me even slower. Each step it took, my spine shivered in fear. I wanted to run, but I had no control of my body. I couldn't scream for help, I couldn't beg for mercy, I couldn't even yelp in fear. I just stood there. Eventually the demon came face to face with me. It towered over me like a bear over an ant. I saw steam come straight out of its nose like a chimney. The heat radiating from it, it was so hot that my body started to roast, turning more red with each passing second. Its mouth opened slowly to show its massive yellow swords for teeth, stained with the blood of humans and animals it's eaten.

I stared right into its mouth, mesmerized from the small autumn glow in its throat. I knew it was the flames of the Dragon, the same flames that destroyed this world. However, I wasn't afraid. For some reason, that glow was so calming, I just couldn't look away. The glow grew so quickly as did the heat of it. I could feel it start to boil my skin as it became a fiery blast. Just as the flames were about to overwhelm me, I heard a quiet, crackly voice whisper one word.

"*Survive.*"

I opened my eyes and saw I was still in the cave, still on my knees as I was at the very end of it. I looked at my left wrist, and though it was tough to see, I could tell my scar had gotten worse. The black scar had spread past my wrist and started to work itself past my elbow. Though there was still no pain, it could be messing with my blood and body in other ways. I looked at my hand, and I saw I was holding a vibrant blue rose. The light from it was still bright but not nearly as blinding as it was before. Why was this rose radiating such brightness that it could probably blind someone by the sight of it? Why did it change colors? What was that vision I saw? Who was that man, and what did it all mean? I'd never heard of a flower in any story or tale that changed colors, and this was clearly a rose. I knew this flower had something to do with my powers; somehow they were connected to each other. I also knew there would be no answers to my questions if I stayed there, but as I started to head back, I saw a little crevice in the end of the cave, a hole.

It wasn't anything massive, just big enough to fit my hand through but enough to escape if I moved some of the rocks and dirt around. At least, if I wanted to. What would I gain from escaping? If I fled, it wouldn't be too long before they noticed my disappearance, and they'd go to the only place I could go. No, I couldn't run away, not until I had secured my town's safety and freedom.

I start heading back to the army, back to Augustus. It took me a few minutes to get out of the cave; each step I took I was able to rise just a little bit. It wouldn't be too long until I was back on my feet walking out and heading straight to the *emperor*.

"This was causing the light in the cave," I said as I placed the flower in front of him.

He grabbed the flower, and it immediately started to shift colors. It went from royal blue to bloody red. Many flashes passed me by, it wasn't like what I saw in that cave; they were glimpses. It all passed me quickly. Some I couldn't tell, but there were three that stayed for more than a second. I saw an old man lying on the ground, a knife impaled in his gut, his white cloth drowning in blood and his golden cross being ripped off his neck by a faceless figure. I saw a man in the bottom of a ship on his knees, like he was offering himself as a sacrifice. I also saw coming out of the shadows a devious smile, the rest of his face still shrouded by the darkness, but I saw his white teeth and his venomous purple eyes. Finally, I saw a knight in white armor racing across an open field filled with men fighting each other on horseback, wiping out droves of men with one swing of his sword. Could that... could that be Augustus? The flashes finally ended as we both dropped the flower immediately. He turned his head to me and most likely stared at me with disgust in his eyes.

"What the hell was that?" He spoke to me with a sense of hate coming from his voice.

"I don't know. It was white in the cave, and it transformed when I touched it," I responded, picking up the flower from the ground. As I lifted it from the ground, I paid close attention toward the radiating flower, a dark red light coming off it. After a few seconds of me holding it, the light slowly faded away, dying along with the flower. The leaves turned old and dry, the red getting darker, and eventually, the flower went limp, the light gone from it. I held it up to Augustus as if I was offering it back to him, but he just stared at it, probably with disgust.

"I guess that's that with it," I said to him as I started to walk back to the twins with the flower.

"Azul," he said. I turned my head back to him. "I hope for your sake and the sake of your people that you know it'll take more than a simple task to be truly a part of this empire."

"Like I told you, I'll do whatever it takes to save my people... my lord," I said as I walked back through his legion of obedient dogs.

CHAPTER 11

Our march was put on hold after I brought the flower to Augustus. Maximus told us to make camp next to the cave. There wasn't a clear spot for us to set up, so we were scattered across the thick forest. As we were setting up, my mind drifted off, thinking about those visions and what they represented. Who was that man, why did he kill himself, what's his link to the Dragon? From what I heard and understood, he was a Muslim and probably Arab. Perhaps he was from North Africa and he was in the massive desert south of the Mediterranean coast. But his eyes, there were as blue as mine. Could it...

I didn't want to get my hopes up. That man couldn't be my father, right? I tried to connect the dots and see if it could work. We were both Muslims but that couldn't be the only thing to go off of. We both had blue eyes. There was very little to figure out who that man was. But why would that flower give me a vision of some random guy? Especially a man who killed himself. The flower had to have given me that vision; the moment I touched it with Augustus, all those visions popped right into my head. Perhaps that man unleashed the Dragon; it had haunted my life for as long as I could remember, and yet no one knew how it came to haunt us. And those three quick visions, were they of Augustus? The last one seemingly was, yet why would this man, with his massive army, fight? He clearly had the strongest army in this region and he had these men on a leash, why would *he* need to fight? Perhaps those visions were just that, visions. There was no way to prove that what I saw was even real to begin with. I wanted to believe that, I wanted to believe it wasn't my father who caused all this pain and suffering. I wanted to believe that Augustus was just a feeble old man, but I couldn't shake the thought that I was supposed to see all that. I took the flower out. It was practically dead, the petals looking as black as the night sky. Yet those petals were all still there, with no change to them besides their color. Could this be the source of my gifts? Could they be trying to guide me? It wouldn't be my best plan to trust some random plant, yet I had no one else right now. I figured I might as well keep it in the back of my mind as I placed it away.

As we finished putting everything up, I noticed that the guard who was watching my every move, Antonio, was sitting beside me. He was eating some form of meat, but I couldn't tell what, a rabbit maybe? He had been silent since this trip started, barely talking to his brother and certainly not talking to me. I decided I may as well attempt to talk to them if I was going to be here for the long run.

"Antonio, where are you from?" I asked him. He lifted his head. He had a disgusted look on his face, like I told him I killed his brother.

"Why do you care, peasant?" he growled at me.

"If I'm going to be a part of this empire, I may as well get to know the people I'll be living and fighting with," I replied to his question.

"And what led to this change of heart; just today you glared at me like I was Satan," he asked.

"I think it's safe to say neither of us cared about the other. I was bitter about being a prisoner, and I doubt you'd care if I died on our march. That said, I realize there's no point in me being bitter with my new reality. I'd say let's try and make the most out of this situation," I explained to him. As much as I wanted to kill Augustus and free myself, I needed to know how he got his men to be so loyal to him, or at least know why they're petrified of him. Antonio stared off in the distance, probably thinking about his home, what he left behind for this life.

"We're from a small town next to the mountain of Viso, once under the control of the Genoan kingdom," he said hesitantly. I didn't recognize the name of the kingdom, but I knew the mountain was near what remained of Italy.

"What made you join this force?" I asked politely.

"Tell me, peasant, are you trying to steal some secret from us?" he retorted aggressively.

"No," I responded kindly and quietly. "I just want to know. I lived in that tiny town you raided. You can imagine how few visitors we got; I want to know why you'd leave what sounds like a peaceful life to fight."

"Well, if you *must* know, that peaceful life is why I'm here, I wanted to escape it," he countered, picking up a small rock and tossing it up as he continued with his story.

"I started serving Augustus just after that damn demon destroyed this continent. I was a young man when I heard his call to action, an opportunity for a greater purpose in life than being a farmer working in a tiny town. A chance to, as he put it, "leave my mark on this continent." It was everything I wanted: to serve my people, bring some honor to my family, as our father died serving in the Genoan army when he was my age," he proudly claimed, looking at the rock now instead of tossing it up. It appeared he was holding it very tight, like he didn't want to lose anything else. At first Antonio seemed like another faceless piece in Augustus's army, but now, it was like his face had been revealed to me, all his details slowly popping up. His face was mostly covered with a beard, but his forehead and nose were reddish pink, his eyes were a greenish brown, and his hair was short and black, fairly receding but still mostly intact. His face was a bit chubby, but nothing too major as his nose was fairly sharp. He was a big man, I knew that, but his size didn't come from just his armor. He was naturally large, no major muscles but just a huge lad.

"I'm sorry about your father. He sounded like a good man, may he rest in peace," I said, offering my hand as a way to console him. He looked at it and then waved it off.

"He was, and I know he is. He died for his people, for his nation; there's no better death than that. Once I heard Augustus preach those words, me and Razul left the town and started our march with them. When I left, this right here," he said as he pointed toward the many tents surrounding us, "this became my new country, my new family. We choose to work together to create a new Europe, one better than the old one. For the people we left behind." He spoke like a man of pure conviction. So, Augustus had been involved in European politics for at least twenty years. It made sense given how wide he claimed his empire was, not to mention how old his son was. Maximus seemed like he was around twenty-five, give or take a few years.

"Through blood and iron," I said coldly, my eyes stuck on Antonio, curious to see what his reaction was, which turned out to be a simple shoulder shrug.

"Yes, we had to kill some people, but for every town we've conquered, they've found themselves to like our rule over the savagery they were stuck with before us. That right there, making a difference, making a world where the weak aren't bullied into submission but where our civilization can rise and come back stronger than ever through the hell we've endured... That's why I fight. For my child whose face I haven't seen, for my wife who's been out of my reach for ten years. I do this for them, for their future," he said, choking up on his last words. I ventured back to my previous feelings about this army. Perhaps my gut instinct was wrong. It might just be Augustus who's the true culprit, not the men who followed his orders. Based on the few I've talked to, it seemed like they weren't bad at all, certainly not on Louis's level. I might be jumping the gun though; there were thousands of these men, surely they all couldn't be saints... right?

"Have you thought about leaving this behind, going back to your family and building a life for them?" I asked, placing my hand on his shoulder to support him.

"I have a few times; each time I couldn't will myself to do it. As much as I care for them, I can't abandon these men. They have a special place in my heart," he said to me. I could hear the anguish warring with pride in his voice.

"Thank you, Antonio. It must've been tough for you to remember what you left behind and bring those emotions back," I replied with a hint of gratitude in my voice.

"What about you, what made you choose to rebel against... what was his name?" he asked me. The question felt honest and genuine, but I still felt a bit of hostility in the tone.

"Louis," I gave him the answer to his own puzzle. "My..." I was about to say father, but as the thought came to my mind, his final words rang in my head like a bell. I took my hand and rubbed my face, trying to get some peace in my own mind. "The man who raised me, Louis was beating him to death. I couldn't stand back and do nothing, regardless of how afraid I was. I took a blade and cut his head off," I replied, much to his surprise given the look on his face. He looked at me as if I was some monster, much to my discomfort. I tried to take the conversation away from myself.

"How did your town become loyal to Augustus?" I asked abruptly. His shocked face slowly reverted back to what it once was.

"My town swore fealty about twenty years ago. We requested men and their loyalty, and they complied. The last time I was there, though, was ten years ago," he said.

"They didn't lay waste to your town?" I asked him with a hint of anger and confusion. Why was his town spared the raid that took so much from my people? I couldn't wrap my head around it.

"From what I remember, the town was given an ultimatum: surrender to the Empire or face us on the field. They took the option of peace. Only a fool would meet a superior force on the field," he said to me casually. My mind went back to Louis and Russell, both there as servants for Augustus, both there to *keep the peace*. Perhaps it would've been better for me to accept that reality and accept Adam's fate. The thought disgusted me; I could feel the apple I ate recently coming back up my throat, though it never made it all the way. I shook my head to remove that revolting thought out, barely believing I allowed it to fully form, not to mention even thinking it in general.

"It might be foolish, but I don't regret my decision," I said to him with pride. "I'd rather die defending the man who raised me than let someone put their hands on him."

"On that, we agree. Family above everything, and you followed that mentality, pe... girl," Antonio said, extending his hand to me. I stared at it for a bit, almost afraid that it might be some trick that he was playing on me, but I inevitably shook it.

After my talk with Antonio, and once Razul returned, I started to venture around the camp with the supervision of my two guards. I found myself walking to a roaring crowd of men, screaming and hollering at each other. They were watching something, or someone. As I got closer, I could hear them chanting names, one of which was Maximus and the other was a soldier by the name Leonardo. I pushed my way through the crowd until I found myself in the front of a ruckus crowd and saw what the two were doing, wrestling. The match was reaching its peak from what it seemed like. Leonardo had wrapped himself around Maximus like a spider his prey, and was choking him out. The crowd was screaming Maximus's name deliriously, feeding the prince as he started to rise up. Leonardo used all his strength to keep him down, forcing Maximus to fall back to the ground, but it appeared to only fuel the prince even more as he continued to fight, much to the delight of the crowd. As soon as Maximus got on his feet, he immediately threw himself onto the ground back-first, crushing his opponent. The crowd of drunk men went wild at the sight of that, screaming and hollering as Maximus took the advantage. He wasted no time grabbing Leonardo's right hand and leveraging it between his legs, causing Leonardo great pain. The bloodied soldier had no chance of escaping and started screaming out mercy to Maximus and to a thunderous roar. Maximus rose, first in a stumble, but he eventually got his balance together, raising his hands to the roar of the crowd. He helped Leonardo up, and the two hugged each other.

Leonardo walked back to his tent gingerly. He was a large man, about the size of Maximus but with more muscles. His body was covered with scars, which I took as proof he had been fighting for a while. Maximus took a beer from someone's grasp and drank the entire thing in one gulp, chucking it behind him to a roar of the crowd. It was deafening how loud the Maximus chants were. The crowd eventually started to die out as the fight had ended. Most of them went back to their tents or to their fires to warm up. I decided to stay there and talk to Maximus, to get some questions off my chest. I walked up to the mud-covered man who was talking to some of the men in the shrinking crowd. Once he saw me, he told the men there he'd meet with them soon and headed my way.

"Quite the show you gave them," I said to him. He chuckled as he started to wipe the dirt off him.

"Well, it's always good to have a great bond with your men, and Leonardo there was claiming no man could beat him. I just needed to humble him," he replied with a bit of cockiness in his tone.

"Is this something you do often?" I asked him.

"It may not be wrestling, but these men are my brothers. If we can't act like brothers, then we're just some loosely organized mob," he responded with pride.

"You actually care for these men, don't you?" I said, slightly shocked. He looked slightly hurt by the comment.

"Of course, I do. How could I not care for these men who've put their trust and lives in my hands? Each of these men would die for me, and I would do the same for them."

"For a better Europe," I said, almost like it was a question. "What's the point of this invasion, Maximus? Surely it isn't about the money or the land. Why is your father wasting so many resources to attack this town?"

"You said it yourself, a better Europe. One that's completely united under a common banner. One that is no longer bickering amongst itself for petty issues like land or which lord controls what resource," Maximus proclaimed proudly, wiping the mud off his forehead.

"That can't be the only reason, though, right?" I continued to pick at his answers, wanting more from him.

"Maintaining order and stability; if one town within our empire chooses to break off from our rule, what'll stop others from doing so and causing a full-fledged mutiny." With that, he started to walk back to the crowd.

"Maximus," I said quickly to get his attention once again. He turned toward me, clearly giving me all of his attention, as I walked up to him. This question wasn't for anyone else besides him.

When we were right next to each other, face-to-face, I said, "What's your *true* goal? I know this better Europe comes from your father, but what do you want?" I wasn't sure if that's how I wanted to ask him, but the cat was out of the bag. His face was stern as he mulled over the question, waving off the men who were still waiting on him.

"That goal is one that my father has had for years, yes, but that doesn't mean it's not my goal too," he finally said.

"I know that, but I want to know what do you *truly* want?" I repeated after his quick answer. I don't know why I was so desperate to know this; Maximus wasn't a target of mine, nor should his dreams and goals matter to me. Perhaps I just wanted to learn more about this man, know what made him tick. Perhaps I was just curious. Either way, I was in too deep to simply walk away without more than some basic answer.

"What I *truly* want," Maximus repeated to himself. "There's a lot that I want, a lot of dreams and desires and goals. I want these men to return home to their families. As the crown prince of this empire, I want to be the greatest ruler this continent has ever seen. I plan to rule with a soft but firm hand, and above all else, I *will* be the one to save this continent."

"Those are good goals. I hope you do achieve them, my lord," I replied back. He motioned for my guards to leave us and waited until no one was around or watching us. He took another step, so that we were right in each other's breathing space.

"I don't think you fully comprehend, Azul. I don't mean save this continent from robbers and men claiming royalty in their blood, I mean from the Dragon. I will be the one to free us from that beast's reign in the sky. I *will* tame it, or if I cannot do so, I *will* kill it. I hope that answered your question," Maximus whispered to me, turning around and heading back to his tent.

It did, and it shocked me to hear what he thought. My mouth was frozen, and I couldn't say anything. I wanted to ask how he could think such a thing, why does he differ so much from his father, and more, but I couldn't. I started to walk back to my tent; each step I took I thought about Maximus and who he was. He seemed to be a better person than his father, but it was more than just his goals and how he treated me. He genuinely cared for the people he fought with and seemed to be a kind man. These soldiers weren't just blood-crazed maniacs but people who had their own reasons to fight for this army and serve Augustus. Perhaps in a different time, I would've bowed to them as my lords, but not now, not when the blood of my people still laid on their blades.

I went back to the tent Maximus promised me, and as I entered, I saw an armored man waiting inside. It took a second for me to realize it was Augustus who stood in the middle of the tent, staring right at me. As he waved my guards away, I felt my gut get wrapped up together; his presence caused my blood to freeze, and my body shifted from a simmer to a frozen tundra. Why was he here, why did he want me alone? Was he going to kill me? Why was he still wearing his armor? He looked almost like a shadow, the flames from the outside barely lighting his white armor. Without it, I could barely point him out, the way I presumed he wanted it to be.

"Before you speak, girl, I want you to listen," he said quietly. I saw no reason to ignore his request. It appeared he wasn't here to harm me, at least I thought so. "Though you did well today surviving the march and volunteering to serve, like I said before, it takes a lot to earn my trust." I nodded my head in agreement—again, no need to be spiteful. *Remember your goal, Azul*, I thought to myself.

"That said, once you've earned my trust, it's permanent, everyone here in this army I trust with my life," he said with a hint of pride in his cold voice. "I'll be blunt with you, girl. I believe that you can be integral for my empire, and I rather you be an ally than a foe, so if you wish to return home, I suggest you do what you have to so you can earn it."

"And like I told you, my lord, that's all I care about, keeping my people safe, so I will do all I can for that," I replied quickly. He nodded his head in approval.

"Good, then before I leave, I have one last question. When you grabbed that flower, did you see anything?"

I wasn't prepared for this. I mentioned it to no one, and I figured it was connected to my own powers, so why would Augustus ask this? Did he have his own set of gifts? Whenever he was around, I did feel this weird energy. Perhaps it was menacing, yes, but nothing about him told me he had any gifts like mine. Given how often my powers overwhelmed me, the fact it hadn't with him should be enough proof that he was normal. When I've tried to summon and channel my powers, I haven't noticed his energy at all.

"I've been around a long time on this earth, and I've heard many witches and soothsayers claim there's certain flowers and artifacts that'll give those who wield it visions and powers," he quickly replied.

"Do you believe those soothsayers... my lord?" I asked back to him, hoping to get a bit more out of him and what he believed and knew.

"Before the Dragon, I'd probably kill them for heresy and their pagan thoughts but with that monster in the sky, their schemes are a risk I'm willing to deal with," he said in the same cool tone, like nothing could phase him. I thought long and hard about what I should say. Should I be completely honest, or should I lie? He might not have seen anything; perhaps it was linked to those with gifts? Or perhaps the visions were for all.

"I'm afraid I couldn't tell what I saw, my lord. There was something flashing before me, but it moved so quickly I just couldn't decipher it," I revealed to him, to which he shook his head.

"Thank you for your honesty. I figured as much since that's what I saw too," he told me, placing his armored hand on my shoulder. The steel felt like ice was touching my bare flesh despite the layers I had on. It took all of my self-restraint to not cut his hand off. "And just like that, your dream of returning home is a step closer to you."

"Thank you, my lord," I said humbly to him, wondering if now was the time to strike. Against what might be my better judgment, I chose not to.

"Goodnight, child, we have a long day ahead of us," he declared as he left my tent, leaving me to my thoughts. He was testing me; he wanted to see what I would reveal, if I was trustworthy, and I passed. Maybe he was lying, maybe he knew nothing, and I gave him knowledge he wouldn't have access to. I doubted it, though. He had been as straight forward as anyone I'd met; if he wanted to lie, he'd had plenty of chances to do so. Maybe heading home wasn't too much of a pipe dream. Or maybe he was just filling me up with false dreams only to crush it. Regardless, he was right; we had a long day tomorrow, and I needed to rest. I put my head down on my bed for the next day.

CHAPTER 12

The night after my talk with the emperor and prince was long and filled with no peace. I barely slept, no matter how hard I tried to. I was haunted. As I finally started to fall into a deep slumber, all I saw was death surrounding me. At first, I relived Adam's death all over again, then the invasion haunted me, the bangs of their guns going off, tearing my eardrums apart. It felt like my sanity was being plucked away each time I closed my eyes. The third time, I only saw the visions from the flowers again, only more intense. I could feel the burning heat and sand scratching my face. The whispers of the man were louder, and despite the powerful wind, it was all I heard. The screeching calls of "*Lā 'Ilāha 'Illā Allah, Muḥammadun Rasūl Allah*" and "*Ya Allah eaqib aladhin zalamuni wahfazhum...*" drowned my ears. When he stabbed himself in the gut, I felt it in my own gut as I screamed out in pain and agony, falling into the desert's boiling sand. I kept falling until I was alone in the dark. Eventually a figure emerged. It was Augustus, holding a sword in front of my throat as I lay there, beaten and broken. I could feel myself being lifted up, like I was being dragged toward my execution, and as I stood in front of him, I could feel a cold sword pierce my heart, with the following words whispered behind me: "For a better Europe." I turned my head and saw it was Maximus who plunged the blade. He took out the sword, and he and Augustus started turning into smoking figures, only for the true threat to emerge, the Dragon. That's where I finally woke up, covered in sweat and short of breath.

It was still the dead of night. I popped my head out of my tent and saw there was no one out there—a few torches still lit, and it appeared a fire near the center, but no one was there when I checked. As I went back inside my tent, I looked at my left hand. The scar was still the same size, yet when I felt it, it was like I was touching the dirt. The scar didn't change, nor did it break up or shift, much like how if I touched my right arm, it wouldn't change, yet the fact it felt like dirt concerned me. I sat up and tried to meditate, trying to put calm thoughts back into my head. My mind ran back to that river near my town, how the cold water felt on my skin, how my life was like before Augustus ruined it. I could feel the warm air on my face and flowing through my hair. I could feel the grass in between my toes and under my feet. I felt this sense of calmness surrounding me, peace within myself. That peace was short-lived as the sounds of the horn blasting woke me up. I opened my eyes to see that the shroud of darkness that surrounded us now had a gleam of light in the sky. I touched my left arm again, and the dirt-like feeling was gone, and along with it, the scar shrank. Perhaps it was just actual dirt that was on my arm, maybe some of the mud from the wrestling match splashed on my body while I was watching.

We didn't have a lot of time to prepare ourselves for the march as the screams to hustle broke any semblance of peace after that horn erupted. I had no idea why we were in such a hurry, we supposedly had two days left of our march, and we were making, in Razul's words, "great time." Though I heard from some of the men as we grabbed our food that we had to reach some rendezvous point. We quickly ate whatever we could and then lined up for our march to begin, much to the disappointment of some of the men who complained about the lack of food and how they were running low on rations. I wasn't hungry at all; I imagined this was another side effect of my gifts. Since they healed my wounds, it could be allowing me to survive without food.

The marching felt easier today; my feet had grown stronger from the constant walking, and I wasn't as exhausted as I was from yesterday. As we marched through the forest, I tried to hone my gifts. I slowed my pace down a bit, just enough that I was still moving with the group but I could focus on my own mind. I closed my eyes briefly, trying to calm myself down and retrieve that strength. I could feel my heartbeat slow down; my breathing went from rugged panting to a cool pace. I felt my legs get a jolt of power, like my blood was replaced with pure energy. With each step I took, I felt the strength coursing through my veins, giving my legs a boost they so desperately needed. It wasn't much, perhaps a small shock in my system, but enough to know it worked and I was building on my training from before. The day passed quickly. I probably could have gone another few hours, but the rest of the men were exhausted. While they took breaks throughout the journey, I would meditate, channeling all that energy toward my heart. By the time we made it to the rendezvous point, the sun had set a while ago, and the stars were shining in the sky.

As we set up camp, I noticed that "my personal guards" were swapped for a new man— Richard, I believed. He had my blade and looked very similar to Antonio, though he had a scar across his face and was the same size as the other two. Perhaps Augustus—or more likely, Maximus—had some faith that I was growing into his family. I laughed that idea out of my head. Two days had passed since the attack; I highly doubted he would be that trustworthy. As we finished placing our separate tents, I felt compelled to talk to the young man.

"So, where are you from?" I asked. The man never looked over, still focused on tying up the last parts of his tent.

"Up north, near Paris," he said coldly with a thick French accent. It was weird hearing that accent, nearly everyone I talked to didn't have it. Perhaps it was because we were so close to the remains of Spain, the accent was less common; perhaps we have a mixture of the two accents in my town. I ran into it once or twice, but it seemed so foreign to me. Paris also seemed foreign, like a fairytale city from what Adam taught me. The center of France and the height of culture on the continent. It was a shame that the city was torched to the ground.

"How did you join this army?" I asked kindly and quietly.

"The same way most of these men joined, I was given a choice to fight for something bigger than myself and make some decent money for my family," he said bluntly. "All it cost was leaving them." Forced conscription, a *brilliant* way to beef up your army and build some sort of common bond among the troops. And I guess another common bond among the men were the families they left for this force.

"Was it worth it? The money and what you're fighting for. Is it worth not seeing your family?" I replied to his response. He took a deep sigh and stared at the tent for a few seconds, just doing nothing.

"Their protection and security make it worth it," he said in a sad tone, like they were in his heart, but it still hurt thinking of them. "Knowing that they're safe and no harm will come to them, that makes it easier to deal with not seeing them."

"What do you think of Augustus?" I asked him after a couple of seconds had passed. Quite random, but it still felt like I hardly knew anything about my emperor.

"He's a good leader," he said bluntly. No fear in his tone, no shift in it either. He didn't seem like his body changed either; he was either completely enamored by him or he truly believed that.

"Anything else?" I said, trying to pry more information from him.

"There's nothing else that matters for me, girl," he stated, shutting the topic down. "I've been a part of this army for ten years, the only thing I care about is making it to the next day and eventually returning home."

"What about Maximus?" I said without much thought, and in an instant, his face lit up.

"Maximus, he's great. What about him?" he said back to me with passion.

"But what about him makes him great? I barely know him, and I know I'll eventually serve him, but I'd at least like to know what makes him so great," I replied back to him. He stood there, staring at the ground, and thought about what to say.

"He's a man you'd think God himself created to be a ruler. He's kind to his people, serving them before himself, he's in the thick of the fighting, showing no fear for death. A true king, unlike... someone else," he said, looking down as his once bright face got slightly darker. Was he talking about Augustus?

"Who is that someone else?" I asked. His eyes still faced the ground, not giving me any attention.

"That someone else is none of your concern. I'd die for Maximus, much like anyone here would. He would do the same for us, no doubt," he replied to me, staring into my soul through my eyes. I immediately looked down to kill some of the tension and keep him cool.

"Sounds like a good man," I said to him.

"He's the best man I've ever met. I'm proud to be fighting alongside him. I've heard he once convinced an army of a thousand barbarians to surrender to us by meeting with their ruler and working a deal out. Though, he does have some intriguing beliefs," he proclaimed as he started to gather some food to eat. *Intriguing beliefs?* Could he be referring to the Dragon? I could see Maximus telling everyone his ultimate desire; specifically if they have any information that could help him tame it.

"You mean his belief that he can tame the Dragon?" I asked quickly, to the nodded head of Richard. "How could he think that? That beast is feral and would rather burn your face off than listen to you." He turned his head and once again glared at me.

"Girl, if that man for even a second believes that he can tame the Dragon, I have the utmost confidence that he can," he said deadly and with a cold conviction in his voice. I felt his words hit me like the cold wind would hit my barren skin. "There's a few of us who believe in some of those conspiracies, whether it's from a witch, they get it from a dream or even a book." He said as he finally stood up to go to his bed. Before he walked inside, he turned to me and said this last line. "If there's one thing I know about Maximus, it's that he's the best hope we *all* have for a better future, you included."

He went into his tent, presumably to eat without being bombarded with questions. I looked around to find Maximus's tent. I was curious as to why he would believe such insanity. He seemed smart, and I'd imagined since he was a prince, there'd be no reason for him not to be educated. He surely knew the flaws in his plan. After glancing around, it seemed like most of the men went to their beds, so I decided to return to my tent and contemplate what he said. It was clear that the men hated Augustus, or at least feared him. The reactions of Richard, Arthur, and even of Maximus screamed it out. I didn't have to say his name to know who he was referring to. What I couldn't put together was why, though? I think back to that vision I had. He was a dominant force, or at least I think that was him. Maybe he's still in his prime, maybe they're in line because he worked his way to the top through military might. No, how could he be in his prime when some of these men have fought for him for nearly twenty years? I know he couldn't have any gifts; someone would've let it out at some point. Perhaps it was out of admiration toward Maximus. They fought for his father as they know he'll inevitably be replaced by him. They put up with Augustus out of love for Maximus and given how much these men love him, it made sense.

Maximus did seem like a good man. I imagined my life would be more miserable under the direct control of Augustus and no Maximus. I've never seen this loyalty for anyone. Louis was hated by his men, only surviving due to their fear of him. I could see his bond with the men during that wrestling match, he seemed like a charismatic man, but this admiration made it seem like he was the second coming of Jesus. Perhaps to these men, that's exactly who he was, why else would Richard be so fine with Maximus believing in such outlandish things? Because he believed in his future king, so much he probably looked to him as his god.

As I lay in my tent, attempting to sleep, I heard Maximus talking to my guard. I didn't hear much, but I did hear him talk about "patrol." After my first night under Augustus's control, I noticed at least two men watched over the camp as lookouts. If I wanted to learn more about Maximus, without his goons surrounding us, this was my chance.

"Do you need a partner, Maximus?" I asked while popping my head out of my tent. The two chuckled. I imagined the sight of their prisoner popping up and volunteering to serve was quite humorous.

"I suppose you can join me as a lookout," he responded, taking my blade from Richard and handing it to me. We made our way to the edge of the camp, where there was a fire already sparked for us.

"First time doing this?" he asked, handing me a leather water bottle, to which I drank from, tasting the dirt in it.

"No, I had the privilege of patrolling my town when I protected it. Even on the day you came I was watching over it," I answered back, staring into the cold and dark forest while doing so.

"Oh..." he quietly responded. "Well, to be honest, you may not have been doing a good job patrolling."

"And how did you come to that conclusion?" I said with a bitter tone, my eyes shooting daggers at him.

"Well, you missed the smoke that came from our camp in the forest and the noise that we were making that night. We were surprised to see you were not ready to fight us. At the very least, we were expecting some sort of makeshift wall or men preparing to fire back," he replied swiftly.

"Yeah, well... I was... going through a lot at the time," I said, placing my memories to the side. I just stared in the forest; I didn't want to discuss it. I didn't want to even think about it. The last thing I wanted on my mind or to talk about was those last few days in the village. I had to stay focused on the task at hand. I couldn't afford to let my pain drown me. We sat there in silence for a bit, neither wanting to talk after my answer. Maximus eventually decided to break that silence.

"Azul, on behalf of my men and my empire, I want to apologize for all of the pain we caused you. You didn't deserve to suffer the way you had. If I could change one thing, it's what we did to your town," he said with sadness in his voice. I looked over, seeing him slouched over, head looking at the ground like he's ashamed of himself. "We should've sent an envoy or someone to inform you of what could've happened, provide a peaceful route rather than break your leg and force you to walk on it."

I felt this sense of pity and sorrow coming from him, like the pain I felt when Adam died. I could feel it; he meant it with all his heart.

I didn't need my gifts to know his tone was sincere. No wonder these men loved him so much.

"Thank you for your kind words, Maximus. There's no point in living in the past, though," I expressed to him.

"Perhaps, but it's the least I can do, and based on what I've heard, you seem to be at least merging well with the men," he replied back, looking toward the tents behind us. I felt a slight sliver of happiness in my heart after he said that, like a ray of sunshine hit my face and warmed my entire body.

"You truly are a good person, Maximus, unlike someone else we know," I retorted. I saw a small smile on his face as he turned to look at me, then back at the forest.

"Well, if you're referring to who I think you are, that's simply because you don't know him well enough," he countered. "Sure, he can be harsh, his presence can be quite intimidating, and it's easy to see him as a dictator, especially from your perspective, but he has dedicated everything to building a better world from the ashes left behind."

"Is that why all these men are fearful and loyal to him? For a better Europe?" I asked, pointing at the tents behind us.

"They don't fear him. You might read their unwillingness to give deep answers as fear, but they're simply loyal to him. Their lives have improved significantly, so why would they question their king since without him, all that they've gotten would be worthless," he answered back. I could see how he came to that, and as I think back to the men who answered, most weren't truly fearful. Intimidated? Absolutely, but perhaps he did enough to justify that level of respect.

"All this for a better Europe," I quietly stated, to which I saw Maximus shook his head.

"A civilization that'll stand the test of time and serve God Almighty," he replied back.

I turned toward him, thinking of what he'd said and what I'd heard. Perhaps it wasn't my place, but I wanted to know how he came to such a conclusion.

"Maximus, why do you think you can tame the Dragon? How can you think that the beast that tore Europe can be tamed?" I asked in a calm voice. He sat there for a minute or so, contemplating the answer. Just as he turned to me to respond, we heard the sound of hooves smashing the earth in front of us. It sounded like three horses, maybe four, were coming. I was ready to pull out my sword, but Maximus stopped me. Five men rode in front of us, each on a horse and all but one heavily armored. They all held the flag of the New Roman Empire.

Maximus walked over to them with a grand smile on his face as he started to greet them one at a time, all except the last member. The banter was simple between the men, questions about how they were doing, what the trip was like, and even what they found. He stated to me these were highly ranked scouts of the empire, men who served Augustus's empire by scouting the outer edges of it. They were from the ruins of the Italian peninsula and the northern reaches of the Dutch lands and Denmark. Once they finished their pleasantries, they immediately headed into camp. There was one of them who wore some robe that covered his face, but I saw his eyes for a brief second. They were a vibrant purple, a shade that was familiar, though I couldn't put my finger on it. He looked old and wrinkly, like he rose from the dirt. He and Maximus seemed to be hitting it off well as they walked away, leaving me by myself. I could see that they were heading for Augustus's tent, and two other men showed up to replace me and Maximus. As they entered the tent, they removed their helmets, exposing their skins to be as red as a tomato and drenched in sweat.

As the night went on, the men slowly left his tent one at a time. After some time, only one was still in there with Augustus and Maximus; I believed it was the man with the purple eyes. As the seconds turned to minutes and then to hours, I stayed there, watching, but nothing changed. I sat like a statue watching until I felt a hand on my shoulder. I immediately turned around and grabbed the throat of whoever was behind me. If someone was trying to kill me, I wouldn't let it happen without a fight.

Much to my surprise, I saw it was Sadiq, whose face was wrapped in shock and horror. I let her go within an instant and hugged her, like I hadn't seen her in years.

"I'm so sorry, Sadiq. I feared you were here to kill me. How did you even find me?" I quickly said as I let her go. Her face was calmer; the fear had slowly left, but she still looked a bit shocked.

"I noticed you weren't home for a while, so I decided to track you down through your energy. I followed yours and someone else who had as much power as you. But now that I found you, I'm even more confused. Why are you not home, who are these men, and why are you so scared?" she asked calmly. Her voice and her presence brought a sense of relief in my heart. Something I've missed for a while. I haven't seen her since I was at the lake; I figured since she hadn't called for me or reached out, she was fine. That said, I wasn't exactly communicating with anyone those last few days.

"A lot has changed, Sadiq, though right now I can't have you getting hurt 'cause you're caught with me," I quietly responded, trying to see how I could get her out of here without alerting the guards. She seemed to weigh a ton as I tried to push her aside. She turned to face me with grief yet care written across her face.

"I don't care if it's not safe for me, you're in danger, aren't you?" she replied, to which I slowly nodded my head. "Then I won't leave you, especially when I know nothing about what's happened to you." One look at her face, her eyes starting to water up, her nose and cheeks both red, the puppy dog look she's giving me, and I couldn't tell her off, not yet anyway.

"These men invaded my town and took it over. They claim to be a part of this grand empire with the goal of creating a better Europe. After they took over, they took me as a prisoner. That's why you need to go, Sadiq. It's not safe for you here, and I don't want you to share my fate," I quietly stated to her. She looked concerned but stoic as well, like she was deep in thought over this situation.

"Then we must free you. There's barely anyone guarding the camp; we can easily make it back to the town within a day if we don't sleep," she said as she grabbed my arm, trying to take me with her. Now it was my time to weigh a ton as I sat there, refusing to move.

"I can't leave, Sadiq. If I do so, the emperor will simply return to my town and burn it to the ground, along with everyone there. I need to find a way to save them before I escape," I replied to her. Her stoic face turned more frightened. No doubt her mind was racing, trying to find a way out of this mess. A thought did run through my mind as we sat there.

"You said you were able to track me because of my energy, but there was another powerful source?" She slowly nodded her head. Her eyes had a look of fear in them, as if the news she was about to give me would haunt me.

"I thought it was nothing as I came to you, but now I can feel its true strength, and it dwarfs your power. Even now I can barely sense you; all that I can feel is this overwhelming presence pushing down onto me," she fearfully responded, her breaths passing by short and quickly. She looked around, frightened. I grabbed her hands and tried to guide her breathing, doing long breaths with her to keep her calm.

"Sadiq, nothing will happen to us, I promise you that. I don't care if this person's power dwarfs my own, I won't let them beat us," I proclaimed, using whatever courage I had in my heart. I couldn't let her be worried, not now. "Do you think you can track who here has it? If there's any chance for me to beat this army, I need to know who I might need to beat."

She nodded her head and took several deep breaths. She closed her eyes and sat with her feet crossed. Eventually, she started to levitate, the leaves and grass started to be slowly pushed aside, and I could feel the air start to push me too softly. After a minute or two, she fell down, gasping for air, sweat running down her face.

"I couldn't find anything. It was like this camp is shrouded by something," she replied in a frustrated tone. My mind ran around, thinking of anything we could do. As I stared at the ground, I saw the dead flowers and grass all around us, and a thought came across to solve our issue.

"What if I gave you this?" I replied, pulling out the black flower from my bag. Sadiq looked at it like it was some worthless trash. "When I held this, I had these visions. I think it's connected to our gifts." She looked more convinced. She reached out to the flower, and as we both held it, almost instantly, everything went black. I looked around to see if Sadiq or anyone was there, but all around me was darkness—no camp, no tent, no grass, nothing. I heard screams emerging from a little light to the side. I started walking over, and the screams got louder. Finally, I reached the light to see a few men chained to the ground, red tattoos etched all over them. Standing above the chained prisoners were ten men in brown hooded cloaks, each holding a white rose. The second they looked at me, everything changed to fire surrounding the world and a Dragon pouring it down, destroying these massive cities and towns. As I covered myself in fear of the flames, the darkness turned to a forest near a river. Near that forest was a cave, and in that cave was a little child, brown as the mud itself. The child opened its eyes, and it was purple.

I woke up to Sadiq holding the flower, with it turning vibrant purple. "Did you see what I saw?" I asked her quietly, her mouth was slightly open, her eyes, which hadn't blinked since I came back, looked glazed over and glared at the flower. She eventually came back to me, shaking her head and looking into my eyes.

"I don't know," she replied. "All I saw was fire and destruction. I felt pain and agony and this sense of dread. Eventually, that all disappeared, and I heard the roar of the Dragon emerge from the darkness and then I came here." She studied the flower, grabbing a petal off the rose and looking over it. She eventually returned to her meditation position, closed her eyes, and without flinching, ate one of the petals. Her body was surrounded by a purple light, not too bright to illuminate the sky but enough to cover her skin. She once again rose. This time no wind was pushing the leaves or myself aside. Her face was calm and stoic. The room was silent as I sat and watched her work. She slowly came back to earth and opened her eyes, taking a deep breath as the purple tint disappeared.

"I saw them, kind of," she reported in a dazed tone.

"What compelled you to do that?" I replied, confused. She slowly shrugged her shoulders as she looked at me.

"The flower, when I touched it, it told me to consume a petal to see all I wanted to see. I couldn't see who they were, but I saw the energy of everyone coursing through them. Most were brown, but you were a bright blue. The only other colors I saw were a bright red and a dull purple from the center of the camp," she said, pointing toward Augustus's tent. A thought ran to my head. That vision I had, it must've been Augustus and Maximus.

"Of course," I quietly stated. "Augustus had powers, but once his son became older, he transferred them to him. No wonder the men fear him and are loyal to him; they fear he still has it, but they must not realize what happened." I looked over to the tent, trying to sense anything I could from them. I poured all my energy, all my attention toward it. I could feel my strength getting sapped away as I kept trying to seek out their strength. Nothing. Nothing came out of that tent.

"Listen, Sadiq, I need you to head back to the town—" I started to speak, but she quickly cut in.

"No, I can't leave you with them," she blurted out furiously.

"Listen, I know you want to protect me, but I won't let you put yourself at risk, not when I still need to play their game and figure out how to save us," I replied to reassure her.

"But there must be something I can do to help you. I- I can..." she stuttered, trying to find anything to convince me to let her stay. I gave her a quick hug and looked at her.

"You already did. I know what I'm up against, thank you. I promise you; I will find you, and when I do, our town will be safe and free," I declared to her. She nodded her head in agreement and snuck out of my tent. Without a trace, she made her way back into the forest, into the darkness, leaving me with the wolves I must tame. For my future, for *all* of our futures. I put my head down to rest, as I knew tomorrow would be a difficult day. Yet I couldn't calm my mind to sink into that blissful sleep. Whether it was the fear of Sadiq getting killed or captured,

I couldn't close myself off, now knowing she was at risk, and it was on me. There was nothing I could do to protect her myself, but… I walked out of the tent and looked at the moon. It had been up for a while, and it was more facing one direction than the other. I went back inside, faced east, and closed my eyes, placing my hands in front of me, and began to pray to Allah.

"Ya Allah, I know I haven't been the best of Muslims, but you are the only one I can think of that can help me. Please protect Sadiq, keep her safe, and let no harm fall to her. I know I have done nothing to earn your blessing, but please protect her, for she has done nothing wrong besides knowing me. Amen," I whispered to myself, rubbing my hands to my face. I felt a bit better. Slowly my heart grew to be at peace with Sadiq, as I placed her fate in the hands of Allah. There was nothing else I could do.

CHAPTER 13

"Girl," a voice whispered to me, nudging me forward, tapping my shoulder. "Emperor Augustus wishes to speak with you."

I opened my eyes to see it was Razul. He wasn't with his armor and was barely awake, as he yawned right after talking to me. I looked around and noticed the camp was deathly silent, and there was barely any light around us. I nodded toward him and started to get my gear, but he grabbed my arm.

"He said for you to come with nothing but the clothes on your back," he reported quietly.

I once again nodded my head and dropped my gear as I made my way out of the tent. The man pointed to the darkness that was the forest. When I looked back, he simply said, "Let's go." Perhaps this was my execution, perhaps me and Sadiq weren't as clever as I thought. I doubt it, though. If Augustus wanted to kill me, he had numerous chances to do it by now. Not to mention why would he do it with no audience, make the people know the price for treason or whatever excuse he'd want to use. I had no real dreams or nightmares, and as I looked up, the moon was gone, but there was no sun out. We walked for what felt like an hour, but in actuality, it had been several minutes at the most. Eventually I heard the roaring sound of a gun going off, the birds flying off to the distance. Their flaps and cries broke the silence that came after the blast.

I looked around and saw him, fully suited, staring down whatever he shot at. There was at least three dead deers and five large birds next to him. He turned to look at me, and in an instant, I could feel the atmosphere change, hitting me like a thousand tiny knives stabbing my spine. There was no one around. I turned to see even Razul had started to wander back to his tent, carrying a few of the birds back. Despite the lack of people, it felt like the weight of the world was pushing down on me, eyes watching my every move. I walked slowly to the man. Though I didn't fear death, I feared if he knew what my true intentions were.

"Did you enjoy the show yesterday, or I presume lack of a show would be the better way to ask?" Even though he spoke to me, he paid no attention to me as he loaded the gun up. My nerves clenched up. Was it possible that he knew all along what happened last night? I took a quick breath, *relax Azul*, I told myself. *Even if he knows, I can't play into my fear, that's what he wants.*

"What show?" I said, dumbfounded.

"Your tent, it has a clear view of my tent. I imagine the second those men came, all your attention was on them," he smartly pointed out, looking around the forest like I was barely there.

"My apologies, Emperor Augustus," I said with my head bowed to him. I felt my stomach turn upside down as I tilted my head, but I needed to play the game, no matter how disgusted it made me.

"No, it's quite all right," he replied softly, aiming his gun and firing, shattering the silent air with it. "If I was in your position, I'd probably do the same thing. I presume you're curious of what we discussed in there."

"Is it my place, my lord?" I forced out of my mouth. All this bootlicking nearly made me vomit.

"Usually I don't give prisoners this information, but I suppose I'll make an exception for you. Those men were assigned to travel across this barren wasteland of a world, from Russia to the savages of the lands below us," he said. *Savage lands. Surely he speaks of North Africa and the Middle East*, I thought to myself.

"What were they doing there?" I asked.

"Collecting information, scouting the region, investigating stories we've heard," he reported.

"Like what?" I responded. He stood there, seemingly alone in his thoughts.

"We've heard tales that the Dragon lives in the Sahara, while others claim to have seen him in Spain. One has claimed to me that there's a secret kingdom underneath the world, some claim it exists in the ocean. There were reports that England's slaves rebelled and ruled the island. I've even heard such ridiculous claims that the Dragon can be controlled through magic," he revealed to me. That last one caught my ear; it was similar to what Maximus believed.

"Do you believe it?" I responded, to which it sounded as if Augustus gave a little chuckle.

"None of them provided me any evidence to back their claims, nor did they provide any of the books they claimed held the truth for me to read myself. I don't take the words of men who didn't see it with their own eyes as facts, that's how you can lose everything on a myth," he coldly retorted. I was taken aback slightly by this. If Maximus truly believed he could tame the Dragon, what evidence did he get that would convince him he could? Was he truly convinced, or was that just lies from him and Richard?

"But those are men you trust, men you sent to scout out the region, surely you believe some of what they say," I quietly pointed out, to which he shook his head in disagreement.

"I do believe their tales. I believed them when they told me Europe had completely fallen into the state of chaos we're damned into. I believed them when they told me the towns and villages they visited in this damn wasteland were filled with cannibal savages, and I believed them when they said they are people out there who worship the Dragon. I believe all of that because that's something I've seen with my own eyes," he said, cold as ice, though I could feel some emotional response from him.

His voice was as stoic as ever. He didn't shift his tone or his demeanor. He stayed even keel the entire time. He brought up an interesting point about the Dragon being worshipped. I always looked at it as a satanic beast. I heard rumors, but I never believed it. Perhaps there were some who viewed the beast as a new god wiping away the old world, establishing a new hierarchy off the bones and embers of the old gods.

"I figured everyone believed the Dragon to be a demon. I knew not many believed in religions, but... I never believed they'd look to the beast like that, especially with it being the one that set this all up," I spat out softly.

"Most people think that. There's some who still believe in Jesus and fewer who believe in Muhammad and Allah, and there's a small group of people who view the Dragon as a god who came down to cleanse the earth of sin," he stated, looking at his gun and wiping the dust off it.

"What about you?" I uttered quickly, without thinking. "What do you think about that beast?" I could tell from how his helmet shifted up that he was looking into my eyes, into my heart. I imagined he was a lion, and I was the deer.

"I believe it's what the other animals are, like a dog or a wolf. Something trying to live in its habitat. That beast doesn't know that it destroyed civilization, nor does it understand that its very existence goes against every law of God we know of. Now, are you satisfied with my response, or do you need me to give you something to truly watch over?" he swiftly asked.

"No, thank you... my lord," I said, bowing down to him and heading back to my tent. But as I started to walk back, several thoughts ran through my mind—one of them I had buried in my mind since the beginning of this journey. I quickly turned around and faced him.

"My lord, may I be blunt?" I asked.

Without looking, he responded, "You're curious why I called you out here."

"Yes, but more than that, why did you put Louis in charge of my town? Why didn't you remove him when you learned about his actions? You claim your goal is to create a better Europe, unified under your rule, but where's your proof that it would be better under your rule?" I asked with a bit of anger in my voice. I might've tossed all my work away, but once I started, it was like a wave; it just wouldn't end until it crashed into the land. He placed his gun down, seemingly thinking the question through.

"To answer that first question, I've heard the endless questions you've asked my men about me, your wandering eyes and your thirst for knowledge. Let this be your warning, girl; these men are not here to be bothered by you. These men have given up so much of their life to serve me, the last thing they should be dealing with is some woman questioning all their life choices," he remarked toward me. His tone was cold, and his words were harsh and cut deep. I nodded my head and simply replied with one statement: "Then I'll ask you this, I know you've conquered many towns and rule such a massive empire; how do I know this is truly for the betterment of mankind and not just your own selfish desires?"

"No matter my answer, I have a *sneaky* suspicion you'll twist it to fit whatever image you have of me," he quickly stated, his helmet fully focused on me. He even took a step closer to me.

"Depends on the answer, my lord," I answered back, to which he slowly nodded his head.

"Very well. I come from a long line of rulers who controlled Europe before the Dragon emerged. You can say ruling is in my blood. I aim to remove all the savage rulers who've taken Europe and not only divided it but punished those who wouldn't serve them and put the land back in the hands of those who should rule," he said with as much fire as I've ever heard from him.

"Why not leave it to the people?" I quickly questioned.

"The same reason your town had to be controlled by me, for if one town within my sphere is allowed to be independent, others will strive to do so too. Though some *might* be ruled in good faith, others won't be. This is a world where the strong and cruel control all and the weak and kind are beaten down. Your town was the exception. Many are or would be ruled by men who'd force the people to fall in line under them," Augustus detailed to me. He made a good point but showed his hypocrisy in full display.

"But if you *have* to rule them, aren't you simply saying you're cruel to your people?" I responded, to which he gave me a chuckle.

"Azul, if you really think I'm some cruel monster, do you think I'd be spending my *precious* time hunting for my men. You think these deers and these birds are only for me? They're for the men to eat. It's been a while since they've had good meat. Do you think they wouldn't have rebelled? Yes, you've seen me at my worst, but remember, girl, you rebelled and killed two of my captains, and despite our victory, you still chose to be defiant and refuse to fall in line. Hence my threat, to which I do apologize for, as I lost myself in the heat of battle." He listed toward me, making a quick bow.

"Depends. Perhaps you have something keeping them in line, perhaps you just want to keep your army as strong as possible. Perhaps you didn't lose yourself but instead let your true self out," I asserted to him, never once moving my eyes off him.

"Perhaps, or perhaps it's simply they know that though I can be harsh and my actions can be considered violent and cruel, they know I care for them more than anything else in this world. And I do, Azul, I care for my people and my empire more than my own soul. I want nothing more than to bring us back to a Europe where people can freely travel and trade without fear of being attacked by bandits. I may be violent in my conquest, but desperate times call for desperate measures. We may have gotten off on the wrong foot, but despite that, I care for you and your tiny town more than I do my own personal wealth and joy," he eloquently declared, sounding like he was nearly ready to cry as he finally closed the gap between us, standing right in front of me. "Who knows, maybe if you fall in line, you'll return to your home their protector again, this time serving me."

"Like how you left Louis in my town to torture everyone?" I testified bitterly to him. "You make these claims about caring so much, yet you *chose* to leave that monster with us."

He took a second to think his statement over, by this point he was right on top of me, his eyes covered in darkness, his suit reflecting the light of the sky onto me. Despite the fact I could barely see, I wasn't going to back down.

"When I came through your tiny town fifteen years ago, Louis was already in charge. I didn't waste time trying to attack such a tiny place; I simply sent a messenger with a letter informing him of my bargain: serve me and you'll stay in control, refuse and die. As you can tell, he chose to serve me. He rode out into the forest a lord and came back a servant of my empire," he coldly stated.

"Why not replace him, why keep him in charge?" I continued to press him. I wasn't satisfied with his answer, not in the slightest.

"What do I gain from that? That buffoon already had the town. I had no interest in wasting resources fighting him if he'd give it up peacefully," he responded quickly.

"So, you knew nothing of his actions, nothing of who he was?" I retorted nervously.

"All I knew is what was told to me. I don't micromanage my captains' towns. If there were issues, they could reach out to me," he said with no emotions.

"But there was no way for us to know who our true ruler was, not to mention how to reach you," I said, practically pleading with him.

"You might not have, but did you not remember that old man? He knew who his true king was. When there's a will, there's a way. I have no doubt someone there could've gotten information to me," he replied to me. I looked down; the sting of my defeat hurt even more now. If I took this man by his word, I truly let those people die for nothing.

"That said, if there's one mistake I made, it's allowing him so much power with so little oversight as you were on the outskirts of the empire. Had I known of his actions, his obsession with banning the Gospel, or in you and your father's case, Islam, I would've replaced him, and he would've been swiftly punished. Now, is that a sufficient answer?" he said with a slight change in his tone, a bit of compassion in it.

"Yes, thank you, lord, but how did you know my father's faith?" I said with what felt like a frog stuck in my throat.

"Simple, I've seen you use the misbaha. I know that's connected to Islam, not to mention I heard from the old man that your father was a devout Muslim, so it wasn't too difficult to figure that out," he replied quietly. As I started to walk, he quickly mentioned my name one last time. "Take two of these deer to the camp and place them in the middle. Razul will know once he sees them to get the rest with his brother," the emperor declared as he grabbed his gun and turned his attention back to the hunt. The deer weren't too heavy once I focused my strength to picking them up. The walk was short, and by the time I came back, Razul was there with his brother, plucking the birds' feathers off and getting them ready to be cooked. And there I stood, confused on all I'd heard and digesting it all. Perhaps Augustus was still all talk, or perhaps I was truly in the wrong place this entire time.

CHAPTER 14

The next day came and went with barely anything occurring. The men left as soon as they arrived, no trace of their existence other than my memories. We began our march with no mention of what they discovered or who they were. The march toward our destination was quiet yet faster than usual, at least, that's what Razul said when we finished. We cracked about thirty miles, placing us less than a half a day's march from the town.

My strength might've sped up the day, as it felt like for every step I took, we passed twenty feet. My feet would've bled from all that walking less than a week ago, yet I felt no ache or pain. My legs were numb after the first day, yet now they're stronger than ever. I could've gone all night marching if needed. My strength had grown significantly since I fought Louis, at least twice from what I felt, just from all this marching. I had much better control as I could use small doses of power without a thought, yet it still took my complete focus to unleash all of my power.

We made camp right next to the river we'd followed from our first day, a way for us to stay on the right path and fish if needed. We were running a bit low on food, yet thanks to Augustus, there was enough meat for all to eat during breakfast. Luck has seemed to shine upon me as I can rely on my abilities to keep my hunger at bay. I could go the entire day marching, and though I'd be starving at the end, if I just sleep, I would wake up like nothing occurred. Many of the men chose to fish, all of which spread across the lake so they wouldn't steal from each other. For the most part, the soldiers kept to their usual groups: the horsemen spoke to themselves, the foot soldiers were joking around the lake, and Augustus was in his tent, I presumed putting the final touches on his plans for the town. As we spread out, I checked my arm and still, the mysterious stain hadn't grown nor gave me any pain, however that didn't remove any concern from my brain.

I spent my day with the men at the lake fishing—for the most part, it was spent in silence. There was the occasional kind word shared among the men, a few jokes tossed at each other, and cheers for whoever caught a fish. Eventually, as the darkness of night started to cover the blue sky, we went back to our tents and shared the fish among each other. There was a small feast among us with plenty of fish from today, week-old bread, leftover deer, and as much mead as one could drink. As the feast got more raucous, the men started getting crazier with every sip they took, singing songs of their old life, their old home, the people they loved, from the children they never saw to their wives. It was a funny yet beautiful sight to behold, these hardened warriors drunkenly screaming about the love of their lives. Some tears, hugs, and laughter were shared throughout the night.

As I left the campfire, many of the men had gone to bed besides a few drunks who were by the fire and the sober men who patrolled around our camp. I started to walk over to my tent, and I saw Maximus sitting on a tree that had fallen over, watching the forest and the sky above us. He must've been there for a while with his plate from dinner still there.

"How long have you been out here for?" I asked as I walked up to him. He moved the plate so we could both sit next to each other.

"Not long after the sun set on us," he answered politely, turning his face from me to the skies after his answer.

"I had a few questions to ask you... my lord," I said to him. I felt less awful calling him lord today than usual.

"There's no need for titles or labels, Azul, and I'll happily answer your questions," he joyfully responded.

"Very well, why are you convinced that you can tame the Dragon?" I asked Maximus bluntly, to which he responded with a chuckle.

"I see you like to take matters by the horn and not waste time," he retorted back at me, turning his head toward me.

"There's no point in dancing around the bush, and since you're my prince, I think it's fair to understand how you could think such a thing, that you could possibly tame such a beast," I responded, almost mockingly, like he's a fool for believing it. Of course, if he actually believed it, there was reason to view him as a fool. He looked up in the sky, no doubt contemplating his answer.

"I knew a bishop from the old Holy Roman Empire; his name was Abraham. He claimed to have read books from the ancient world, testimonials from the Chinese, Mesopotamians, and Egyptians that spoke about these ancient beasts that were locked away thousands of years ago. Based on the details and the descriptions, they were clearly talking about the Dragon. Each book described the beast perfectly except for the color, for one claimed the Dragon was white like the clouds, another claimed it was blue like the sea, and the last claimed it was green like the grass our feet stand on," he said quietly but filled with passion. "Perhaps the Dragon changed color based on how old it is, or perhaps it had numerous children, all of which haunted the earth at some point. According to him, those books claimed the beast once walked and served humans and that it would follow the path of those who have a heart without conflict and without selfish desires." He spoke with such pride and confidence, no doubt, he believed every word from that bishop, but I wasn't sold.

"So, one priest claims to have read books from the ancient world, claims those books have some knowledge about the Dragon, told you some vague prophecy, and you believe it?" I asked with heavy doubt in my tone.

"Those ancient worlds were the premier civilizations of their time, and they were far enough from each other that they couldn't conspire with each other. The Mesopotamian city-states knew nothing about the Chinese dynasties, the Egyptians were stuck in the Sahara. It would've been nearly impossible for them to know what the others knew. Not to mention their accurate descriptions of the beast proves that Dragon at least existed and lived among humans." He pointed to me.

"Do you perhaps believe he was lying to you? Perhaps he never went there or perhaps those books aren't real or that he has them, but he can't understand what they say. Why do you trust him?" I asked with less doubt but still not sure what to make of his claim.

"The old man provided me with the books and translated each one for me from Arabic, as the Arabs, before their civilization was destroyed, had the largest collection of books in humanity. The House of Wisdom as it was called, held books from Spain and Africa to Japan and China. They spent decades translating them and converting them to Arabic. Because of this, if you simply knew Arabic, like he did, you'd know the history of the world," he said to me quietly, but his tone was filled with faith and commitment. "As for lying, when he heard of the New Roman Empire, he *chose* to meet with us, traveling from Italy to us, as we are the last Christian nation standing, he wanted to serve us and God."

As much as I wanted to mock his logic, he did make some great points. I didn't know much about the other civilizations, but I did know about the Muslims and their empire. Adam would tell me stories about Muhammad, peace upon him, and how he struggled to spread the word of Allah across the pagans in Arabia. He told me about the battle of Badr, and the battle of the Trench. Pierre told me before their fall to the Mongols, the Islamic Empire stretched from Spain to India and was the greatest nation in the world. If they were that far in the East, there was no doubt they interacted with China, probably trading stories and learning from each other. And they existed long after Mesopotamia and Egypt's peak had passed. They gained nothing from lying about their texts and making it up as they went. However, there was one thing I desperately wanted to know.

"Why do you believe that you'd be the one to tame the Dragon?" I said in a tone that was more merciful than before, kinder and more open to reason.

"My father told me about my lineage when I was a boy, that we share the blood of the Roman emperors, the men who created the greatest empire in history. That's why we chose to call ourselves the New Roman Empire, to revive the old ways and bring it back to the world," he proudly claimed. "There's no doubt that if anyone can tame that beast, it would be someone of royal blood. I know how you feel about my father, but I can promise you one thing, my heart is pure. There's no conflict. I'm driven by one thing, and that's creating the perfect empire." He sounded like he was completely at ease with his statement, like nothing could convince him otherwise. I didn't doubt his claim of being a good person, but that alone couldn't be the reason he felt so confident in taming the Dragon.

"There must be another factor fueling you. You can't go off one priest and a book for something this massive," I said quietly.

He sat there for a bit, enjoying the view while he thought of his response, when suddenly Maximus was dragged to the ground and into the darkness of the forest. I immediately grabbed a piece of burning wood from the fire and waved it into the shadow, seeing a massive black bear dragging him from his foot. No matter how much he tried to free himself, the bear held on and took him deeper into the forest. I sprinted right after them. I couldn't let Maximus die. Not only was he a good man, but his death would also be pushed onto me, even if I found his body.

I threw a knife right into the back of the massive beast, which caused it to roar in pain. He dropped Maximus as he stood on its hind feet and turned to me. Its eyes, highlighted in a purple shade, stared right at me. I barely dodged its claws as it swiped at my face. Great, now it wanted to kill me. No time to focus on Maximus. I needed to keep myself alive. I grabbed my sword, but the beast smacked my hand, forcing me to drop it. I felt its massive arms smack me right in my ribs as it frantically swung them around. The blow took the wind out of my body along with nearly cracking my ribs. I could feel the bruise starting to take form, every breath a nuisance for me, as I could taste blood start to flow in and out of my mouth.

The bear started to charge at me, looking to finish the job it started. I grabbed the knife on my hip, the one Razul gave to me yesterday, waiting for the beast to get close enough. As it got right next to my face, I dropped my head from its swinging paw and jabbed the blade right into its left eye. The bear screamed so loud, I thought I would go deaf. It started taking steps back, trying to recover from the damage I dealt it. I saw its black fur starting to turn dark red. Its eye was pouring out blood as it took slower steps around and even stumbling. The bear looked at me with its one good eye, slowly losing its purple shade and fading to a brownish color. If I didn't know better, it appeared to be sad and terrified of me. I nearly put my guard down just as Maximus came through and stabbed the bear right through its head with my sword, killing it instantly. I could see his face was covered with dirt and small cuts, his armor tattered with mud and dents from the rocks. I could even see the place where the bear dragged him. He could barely stand as his leg looked torn up, oozing blood.

I looked at the bear, wondering what would've compelled it to attack us, why was its eyes purple? Maybe a vengeful spirit took over its mind and commanded it to attack, maybe it ate one of those blue roses. I looked around, perhaps someone was around, controlling the beast, but there was nothing but trees and darkness surrounding us. I took my knife and sword out of the bear, and we dragged it back to camp for its hide and meat. It was mostly me dragging the bear as Maximus could barely walk, let alone carry this animal. There wasn't much distance between us and the camp; the bear had sprinted the second he got his hands on Maximus. As we got closer, the chatter from the men grew louder. They started to come near the forest, looking for me and Maximus. They were dumbfounded when they saw us still alive.

"What happened?" one of them yelled. I was about to talk, but Maximus stepped in front of me and spoke.

"This bear tried to kill me, but Azul saved my life," Maximus quickly replied. I had nothing to say, my ribs still stung, and I was trying to regain my breath. The men immediately came to hug and congratulate me.

"That's incredible, Azul. You really showed your stuff," Arthur said as he rushed over to hug me. Their faces of happiness and joy brought the same feelings in my body. It felt like years since I had been happy or even experienced anything close to it, almost like their smiles had removed this thick layer of clouds that hung over my heart and shined the sun's bright light onto me. It wasn't too long for the crowd's roar to grow until it sounded like the entire army was awake and cheering. Eventually, I found myself in the middle of the group, surrounded by their smiles, and it felt so warm, so joyous.

That feeling died quickly as I saw Augustus cut his way through the crowd, looking like a sore thumb with his armor on. Did he fear that he would get cut down by his men that much? That he must always be protected even when he was surrounded by his own mob? What other reason could he have to wear that armor all day?

"What happened?" he said in a tone shaded with concern but drowning in aggression.

"A bear tried to kill me, but Azul here saved me," Maximus said as he put his hand on my shoulder. I couldn't tell due to the darkness and his helmet, yet it felt like, based on his gasp for air, he was about to cry.

"You... you saved my son?" he asked, pointing at me, confused. Like the thought of me saving his blood was such a foreign concept.

"I... I did. It was nothing. I just did what anyone else would do," I responded, now realizing how many eyes were on us, glaring into my soul. The entire army was here, watching us, though their face showed happiness, it felt at that moment like a trial.

"I..." he started to say before he stopped himself. He sounded like he was choking, fighting back his emotions. It took him a second to regain his composure. "I cannot thank you enough, Azul, for saving my son's life," he said as he extended his hand out to me.

I stared at it for a bit, perplexed by what to do and all that just happened. I'd only known the monster that Augustus had shown me. Now, on the verge of tears, he was thanking me? I felt like I couldn't disrespect him, not here, not at this moment. I grasped his hand, he nodded, and the crowd burst into life. He started to walk back, and though the crowd surrounded me, I just couldn't help myself and stared at him. My life had flipped once again, and for the first time in a while, it felt like it flipped for the better.

CHAPTER 15

The night was spent with an even larger party than what occurred during dinner. I knew Maximus was beloved, but for the men to get this crazy again, it was as if the men found their long-lost son. There was a seemingly endless amount of mead and wine to drink, with the men chugging and acting like babies the entire night. I received countless chants, ranging from *Azul* to *Azul the bear killer* to even some *Azul the savior*. I wasn't celebrating as they were, but I did enjoy the festivities—how couldn't I? I was a hero in their eyes. For the first time, I wasn't a prisoner or an outsider. There weren't any harboring feelings of anger or regret among us, there was a sense of unity and family. I cheered with them, danced with them, and even chugged some wine with them. It was a glorious night.

As the party raged into the night and some of the men started to head back to their tents, one of them told me Augustus wished to speak with me. I was surprised since I didn't see him out with us. I also noticed Maximus wasn't out here either, but his leg was messed up, so that made some sense.

As I entered his tent, there was a calming nature to it. It wasn't a pigsty like so many of his men's tents. A few candles were lit, a stack of books with their spines broken on top of his table, and a shelf for his suit and sword. It felt so opposite compared to everyone else's.

"How were the festivities outside, Azul?" he said in a strangely kind voice.

"Oh, you know, it's always fun having a lot of drunk men singing and chanting my name," I said with a hint of humor in my tone.

"That's good to hear, you deserved all the songs and chants you got. What you did was very brave... and once again, I can't thank you enough," he said with sincerity in his voice. Almost as if he meant it.

"Thank you, my lord." Those words were poisonous for me when I met him in the morning, but for some reason, I could say them without wanting to violently vomit. "I did what I think anyone here would do."

"On the contrary, Azul. I don't think anyone here would do what you did, whether it's because they lack the skills or the heart. You're the only person who could and *would* save his life. To be honest with you, I've been thinking about what to do with you for some time, and today, you help solidify my decision," he announced to me while offering a cup of red wine, which I took.

"Oh really, and what has your mind come up with?" I replied as I took a quick sip of the wine.

"I still don't trust you. Three days ago you were a rebel who killed two of my captains, and yet you've done everything you can to convince me that you're loyal. I've seen you interact with the men; you've volunteered yourself when you could've easily sat back, you risked your life for my son. Most prisoners would just die to spite me, but here you are," he said as he walked around his tent, I presumed never taking his eyes off me.

"Well, I've told you all along, my lord, my town's safety is all that matters to me. If serving you means they're safe, I will do what I must," I responded softly. I wasn't lying. I had to be smarter, not only for myself, but for my town. If I acted rashly, I may as well light my town on fire with all of them in it.

"I've been on this planet for sixty years; I've met all kinds of people. I know what you did, the choice you made. They don't just happen, one doesn't swallow their pride like that, not without a plan," he said plainly, questioning my motives. I couldn't let up, not when I was so close to my freedom.

"Well, you and I both know I'm not like *most* people," I boldly said.

"I'm well aware of that. I think I could use one hand to count the amount of rebellions I've faced as emperor, with fingers to spare," he said, practically growling at me. "Though in your defense, you didn't truly know what you were facing."

"Well, to be fair as well, if you were in my position, I'd imagine you'd do the same thing," I responded back to him. It sounded like a chuckle came out of his mouth, but his helmet wouldn't let me see, nor hear it.

"You're right. If I was in that position, I would scratch and claw just to have a horse to ride on," he proclaimed quietly and with a sense of approval.

"I don't trust you, but I trust my son, I trust his mind, and I trust his instincts. As my days on this earth dwindle, my only focus is making him the right man to lead this world back to its former glory," he said with his back turned to me, staring at one of his books. His tone... he ditched the monotone a while ago, but this felt as genuine as anything he had said. He seemed happy and content, and he was just putting it all together here at the end.

"Well, your son definitely has the traits to be a great ruler," I replied to him, looking at his book. I noticed the writing was Arabic, could that... could that be the book that Maximus was talking about, the book from the bishop?

"Since he could walk, I'd done everything I could to train him to be the perfect ruler, a man who his subjects and soldiers would die just to please. I've even thought about surrendering my crown to him and letting him truly rule," he said calmly.

"Why haven't you then?" I asked, finishing the rest of my wine. He shrugged his shoulder as he sat in front of me.

"For one reason or another, I never felt it was the right time to give up my power. But when I die, he will replace me and give Europe a brighter future thanks to the foundation we're building today, and I want you by his side," he said, his helmet directly facing me, as if he were peering into my soul. I nearly choked up on the wine when he said that, coughing and spitting it out.

"By his side?" I tossed back, barely able to believe my ears when he said that.

"Marry him, if you didn't get what I meant," he said coldly.

"No, I understand, but why me? Why not some girl whose father controls some castle, why not a princess or a wealthy woman? Why some common French girl?" I barked at him. It made no sense why he would think I'd be a good candidate for his son. There was nothing about me that screamed empress, nothing about me that screamed royalty, worthy to marry the supposed savior of Europe.

"You just said you're different from everyone I have met here, and you are calling yourself common? You're from this region, you'll be able to unite the people to our empire, under Maximus's rule. Tomorrow you'll march with him alone, as you'll cover more ground that way. You'll convince the town to surrender and once that's done, you'll officially be named the empress of the New Roman Empire, and his wife," he calmly said to me.

"It's not just that, is it?" I pointed out to him. It's one thing if he wanted to unite the French region under his flag, but from what the soldiers had told me, they've practically done that. Other than my town and the one we're going to, France, the lowlands, and the bits of central Europe that weren't scorched by the Dragon already swore loyalty to Augustus. He didn't need me to bring this region together when they're already loyal.

"Your abilities—you possess incredible strength and speed, your children will be a god to these people," he quickly stated. *There it is*. He wanted to build an empire off my blood, off my gifts. Europe's willingness to stay loyal doesn't matter when the emperor, empress, and their heir could crush any opposition into the dirt with their bare hands.

"And if I refuse this *generous* offer?" I asked him. I needed to know what my options were, what was left for me. Maximus was nice, but maybe, just somehow, I could escape to my old life with nothing. He looked around, I could hear a quiet sigh from him, I imagined he didn't like that question.

"Then you've sunk whatever future you had with us. You'll become a foot soldier, mucking around the fields while dragging your life through the cold, wet dirt and dying at the ripe old age of thirty," he said with no charms in his voice, no passion in it, just cold and dry. "This marriage is your only chance for freedom and power, something you can never have if you reject it. This is a gift, you may hate who you're getting it from, you may not like it at this time, but think of it like this, you guarantee your people's salivation, you guarantee your survival and you guarantee a life worth living."

I sat there, mulling it all over. It was an offer I had no business refusing. I got everything I could want: my people protected, my life back in my own hands, and control. I thought of the men outside the tent, the chants they were giving me, the love and admiration they were drowning me in. How could I reject it? Yet I felt this knot in my stomach, this sense of mistrust and dread surrounding me.

"My lord, I would be honored to marry your son," I said with pride. He nodded his head and stood up, extending his hand toward me. "That said, I don't think it would make sense for us to do it tonight nor tomorrow with this task ahead of us. Let us finish what we started and then when we've returned to the capital, we can make it official," I quickly added as I shook his hand. I couldn't toss this offer aside, but I couldn't reject him, I needed to keep this offer within reach.

"I can understand that. Very well, we'll keep this under wraps until tomorrow once you and Maximus accomplish your mission. Now if you don't mind, I need to continue working. You enjoy yourself out there... Empress," he said as he waved me off and went to read the scroll that was on his table.

As I walked back to my tent, I ignored the cries and cheers of the men, the knot in my stomach turned to a death grip within myself, making me feel uneasy and lightheaded. I felt my legs turn to mush as I walked. My clear sight slowly turned to a blurry mess. I stopped hearing anything around me, yet I somehow found myself back in my tent. I guzzled the wine left there and sat down, trying to calm my nerves. *What's happening to me*, I thought to myself. *I have a chance to remove myself from these chains, yet I can't shake this feeling that something's up.* I tried to meditate, to wipe the fears away, but even there, that fear turned to something more frightening. I found myself trapped in a cage, dangling off a cliff from a castle that was black like the night. I was chained up, unable to move, unable to break free. Under my chains, it appeared I was wearing a long white dress, perhaps a wedding gown, torn up and dirty. I felt a tiara on my head, and at the bottom, all I could see were skeletons with the same outfits as myself, dirty dresses with crowns on their heads. I turned to see that Augustus held the chain holding my cage up, laughing through his armor as he dropped me to the roaring sea below.

I couldn't hear my scream; it was a vacuum of noise. I didn't feel myself hit the water, nor the bottom of the ocean; I just fell into the void for what felt like eternity. I woke up screaming, drenched with sweat. I looked around to see that I was back in my tent, lying on the ground. I thought I was by myself until I noticed Maximus was in the tent with me.

"Are you all right, Azul?" he said as he walked over to me with a concerned look on his face.

"Yes, I'm... I'm fine," I said as I wiped the sweat off my face.

"I presume you've already talked to my father, correct?" he asked, taking a seat next to me as I sat up. I nodded my head in agreement. I didn't want to get into that discussion about it, the dream, the proposal, none of it. Yet I knew he was here to discuss it with me.

"Are you afraid of it, what you're asked to do? What this will take from you?" he quietly asked me.

"I don't know, I don't know what I'm thinking at this time, but I don't like it," I replied with my face buried in my hands, trying to gain any sense of peace in my mind.

"I understand, Azul, or at least I think I do. You're scared that you'll be betraying yourself and all you stand for by siding with my father, siding with me," he whispered to me. "You're afraid that by standing by my side, you'll be spitting at all you once held so dear." His tone, his face, his words, they all felt sincere, like he got me, he got my concerns and my fears. I felt I could at least attempt opening up to him.

"I'm afraid that I'll become what I hate, a shadow of what Louis was," I muttered to him. "Or worse, that all of this is just lies placed in front of me, that if I were to be your wife, I'd just be a prisoner with a crown, a false ruler with no power, used only for my blood." I looked to him. His face seemed warm to me. He seemed to be listening and focusing on every word I said.

"I apologize, Azul, for all that has happened to you. You're clearly traumatized by all this grief and pain you've dealt with, and this proposal does nothing to help that pain," he elegantly stated to me. "I know this may be the last thing you wish to hear from the last person you wish to hear it from." His eyes were looking directly at mine as he softly held my hands.

"I do want you to know, when you become my wife, I promise you, you won't be a prisoner. You won't be some false queen; you'd be a true empress. You'd have *real* power within our empire. I'll treat you like the royal highness you are, and I promise you, you'll be given full reigns of your land. It's the least I can do," he declared to me.

That last part, it was like the light of the sun hitting me in the morning. I could finally achieve my promise, protect my people, give them their freedom and safety. The offer sounded like a dream, almost too good to be true. If Augustus told me this, I'd probably scoff at it, believing it to be lies. But it came from Maximus; his words put my heart at ease.

"I... I appreciate your kind words, Maximus, and if I was completely honest with you and myself, I do trust you with all my heart. You've done more for me than you have had any reason to, you've been kind, helpful, and open to me. When you first told me you were a good person, I couldn't believe it, but I realize you truly are one," I said to him, lighting his face up as we embraced for a hug. As we pulled away, our eyes locked, and I felt something between us, something electric. My heart started to beat faster as his face started to blush. So did mine. I felt my body starting to heat up. My stomach started to twist and tie itself up again, this time not due to dread or fear, but for something else.

He went for a kiss. I felt something in me saying to go for it. My heart was pounding a thousand beats a second. As I closed my eyes and went for it, an image flashed in my mind, an image that I had seemingly buried in my mind. It was Charles, dying in my arms as I bawled like a baby. It took me back so quickly, my heart dropped right into my gut. I felt my entire body reject itself as shivers ran through my spine. I pushed Maximus away as I fell back. His face was one of shock.

"I- I can't." I stuttered, trying my best to compose myself, staring at the floor.

"Do you wish for me to tell you how much I care for you because I can if you want," he said kindly, taking a couple steps closer to me, only for me to take those steps away from him.

"No... no, it's not that. It has nothing to do with you, Maximus. I... I still love someone," I said as my eyes started to build up hot tears. I couldn't believe myself. I let the memory of my best friend fade to the farthest space in my mind, coming back only now. I was so desperate to survive, I buried one of the most important reasons I had for survival.

"Keeping your heart locked away for the dead can't be good for you though, no?" he said as he slowly got next to me, placing his hand on my cheek. I held onto it; it felt good as the warmth of it brought back the memories of my time with Charles, how we kissed for the first time, how we spent our time by the lake. I knew I couldn't bring him back, but I couldn't let go of him, not yet.

"You're right, but I still love him. I may fall in love with you, just not now," I said as I wiped the tears out of my eyes, looking into his own eyes. His face lost most of its color, his eyes screamed of depression, and he looked like he saw his family leave him behind.

"Very well, I'll see you tomorrow then, Azul," he said quietly as he walked away. *Great,* I thought to myself. *I just broke his heart, and tomorrow, any chances of earning freedom for me and my town will be dead and buried too.* I simply crumbled to my knees, the pressure of the world collapsing onto me. I could feel the tears pouring down my cheeks. I held nothing back as I sat there, broken. There was nothing else I could do besides let go of my pain and emotions.

CHAPTER 16

The night passed quickly after Maximus came to my tent. I eventually found myself sleeping, after the tears stopped pouring down my face. I don't remember what I dreamt; it was just blackness that I saw. Perhaps it was myself preparing for the dark world I'd be entering, perhaps it meant something else.

Before I left my tent to join Maximus, I spent some time cleaning my blade and staring at Adam's misbaha. The beads were covered with blood, dirt, and scratches, erasing the black paint that covered them. Oh, what I would give to rewind time to before I killed Louis. I put the misbaha around my neck, placed my thin set of leather armor on, and left my tent. There was barely anyone up, and whoever was up wasn't prepared to march either. I walked around, looking for Maximus. It took a minute or two, but eventually I found him walking out of his father's tent. His face still had some of the scars and cuts from yesterday. I looked down to see his ankle had no armor on but a thick cloth surrounding it.

"You ready, my lord?" I said to Maximus. He nodded his head and handed me a leash to one of the horses. I was waiting for some reply, but nothing came as he got on his horse and started to ride. I quickly got on my horse and rode right behind him.

We rode in silence for the first part of the trip, neither one of us wanted to break it, particularly myself. It was uncomfortable and awkward, but I had no interest in talking about last night, as I feared it would only make it worse. I did make quick glances at Maximus. Though he wouldn't admit it, I felt like this was driving us insane.

Anytime I'd take a peek, he would too, probably wondering when I'd talk. Finally, after an hour of riding, I confronted our problem.

"Maximus, I apologize for last night, how I handled myself. I guess the drinks and my mind didn't mix well with me," I quickly spat out of my mouth. I wasn't truly sorry; I wasn't sorry that I still cared for Charles and that I didn't kiss him. Yet we were going to be married, whether I liked it or not. I couldn't afford letting this hang over us. He looked down after hearing my apology, took a deep breath, and then turned to face me once again.

"As much as I appreciate your apology, it is I who should apologize, Azul. I didn't mean to push myself upon you; I felt like there was something and decided to go for it," he said to me quietly, with his sincere voice. I nodded my head back to him calmly, yet on the inside I was surprised, especially as I had already admitted fault. I figured I had to respond in some way to it.

"Don't worry about it, Maximus. I felt something too in that moment, that's why I went for it in that brief second only for... anyway, we can figure that all out once we're done here," I responded, then quickly shifted the topic. I wanted to get as far away from this conversation as possible, so I tried to turn it into a discussion about the town. "So, how will Augustus realize we took the town?"

He pointed to the back of his horse's saddle as there was a small cage with a cover over it. "We'll send this pigeon into the forest; it's trained to find Augustus. He said he'll be forty-five minutes from the town in the forest, safe enough that an attack won't surprise them but close enough to strike quickly should it come to that," he said.

"He really does think of everything, doesn't he?" I said to myself out loud.

"Well, when you've been around as long as he's been, experience becomes more valuable than anything you can think of," he quickly responded.

We spent the rest of the ride in silence. There was really nothing else to talk about; we knew what we had to do. Neither of us felt the need to talk to each other after we got our apologies off our chests.

As we found ourselves out of the major forest, we were able to see the small town, Perpignan, as one of the men called it, a bit ahead of us. The land next to the town was covered with hills, and they lived at the bottom of them.

As we got closer to the town, after each step the horse took, my stomach slowly started to squeeze itself. Though the flag we flew up next to the New Roman Empire banner was white, I feared for the worst. I knew Augustus would have no qualms taking this town by whatever means necessary. The only saving grace I had was that Maximus was with me to try and convince them to join the Empire peacefully, but that didn't calm my nerves. I couldn't shake this feeling that something ominous was going to happen.

As we got closer, I noticed more details of the town. It shared a lot with my own village. The only difference was this small wooden wall that they erected around the town's northern side. On the wall were men pointing their bows at us. Clearly, they felt we were not worth trusting. Did they already know who we were? As we passed the last hill, giving us a clear shot to the town, Maximus rode up in front of me. His white cloak flowed through the air, his suit gleaming in the sunlight, his helmet to the side so his face could be seen by all, he looked like a proper king, a proper hero of old tales. He chose to get off his horse, and as he did so, I heard something cut through the air. It was an arrow coming right toward us. It lost speed and air as it got closer and landed in front of our horses. It appeared to have something wrapped around it; a small note perhaps. Maximus yanked it from the ground and read the note loud enough that the men standing guard could probably hear him.

"We know who you are, and we know why you're here. Leave us now if you value your life," he proclaimed. At least three of the men had their bows cocked and were ready to take our lives. How could they have known who we were and what we were here for? The way Maximus and Augustus spoke, they were supposed to be surprised by our arrival. Perhaps word spread that an army was on the move, perhaps people were by the river and heard our massive army moving. Maximus crumpled the note and dropped it to the ground. He glanced at me before he took a few steps forward, his face was emotionless and contained no fear.

"There's no need for us to go down the path of violence. We wish to talk with you in peace. Please allow us to talk to you, and I guarantee you, you'll like what we have to say," he yelled toward the town.

A few minutes passed after Maximus's declaration. I saw the two archers still facing us, prepared to fire at us. We stood there in silence. Another arrow came flying at us, this one also coming short from where we stood. Maximus grabbed the note on the arrow and read it to himself.

"Let's go," he said to me. The archers on the wall took their bows down but still watched us; no doubt they were looking for any excuse to attack. We made our way into the village, and it was as if I returned home. There was a small center where I imagined most of the trade occurred, a couple wooden shacks as homes, and some farms south of the town in the hills. The only difference was instead of a watchtower, they had a wooden wall to protect themselves. There was no one there to greet us, no army. It was like a ghost town other than the ten archers surrounding us. Eventually a silver-haired gentleman came out of his home to meet us. He wore a bronze chest plate that covered his skinny stomach and a thick black leather top to cover the rest of his body. His face looked like it was made of worn leather, brown from most likely the sun beating down on him and wrinkly. The armor and steel sword on his side made him appear like a warrior, yet given his hair and wrinkly skin, he was clearly out of his prime. The shaggy gray beard also added some age to his face as it covered most of his neck. From my perspective, he appeared to be around sixty years old. People started to flow out of their homes, following his lead. From young children, mothers holding their crying babies, and men holding their swords and tools, prepared to fight for their lives.

"Welcome to Perpignan, I am Raphael," he said to us in a cold tone, glaring right at Maximus. I felt the hatred that came from his words, that came from his eyes, from his face and body language. His voice didn't crack nor did it sound weak, it demanded respect.

"Hello, my sir, my name is..." Maximus started to say before the old man raised his hand to stop him from speaking.

"We know who you both are," he interrupted, turning his eyes toward me, glaring into my soul. How could he know who I am? "We know what you want and how you plan to take it from us. So, I will make my point as clear as your suit, we will not submit to you, you can choose to attack us and force us to live in your empire, but we have no interest in surrendering quietly and living under your thumb."

"My friend, don't be so stubborn. We are offering you a chance for peace, a chance to live under a new, better Europe," Maximus said with the same tone he spoke to me with last night, one ringing with hope and faith. I turned to see Raphael had the same face on; it read as one who could care less about the promises Maximus was making to him.

"A chance to live under another dictator, another king who'll gain all the power and none of the problems that plague us. Your promise of a new Europe is filled with lies and deception. One that just so happens to present yourself with all the power." He scowled at us, venom pouring out of his mouth with every word.

"Raphael, please," I said, damn near pleading with him. "I understand how difficult it could be to find yourself in this situation, one that demands your loyalty from an outside force. But I truly believe this man is trying to create a better Europe. I wouldn't stand by his side if I didn't trust him. I know you don't trust my words as a stranger..." I started to say, but the old man raised his hand to me, to shut my mouth.

"Azul, you were the reason we're in this position in the first place," he said with passion. His statement rocked me to my core.

"How?" I rebutted to him, completely confused by it.

"Your actions inspired us to stand up for ourselves, to not live in a world ruled by these monsters," he said, pointing at Maximus and then glaring back at me. "When we heard your town overthrew your captain, we were inspired to act and overthrow our own dictator, demanding the very same freedom you fought for."

I stood there, contemplating all that had transpired. *Did Augustus know my role in this*, I thought to myself. *Was I being used not just for my powers, but as a tool to crush the revolt I started?* He clearly had men across the continent and enough time had passed from when I killed Louis for the news to spread. There could be even more towns fighting to free themselves after my actions. If we took this town back and word spread that I did it or was a part of it, those towns would return to the fold, further solidifying his power, his empire. As these thoughts ran through my head, I could hear Maximus make his plea toward the old man, his tone slightly shifting at this point.

"Raphael, you don't know me, my father, and you most certainly don't know Azul. I can vouch that we want to see Europe and everyone in this continent prosper under the banner of the New Roman Empire. An empire that will bring the glory of this once proud continent back to where it belongs. An empire where a man can live how he chooses and not be abused by the rich and powerful, by those with strength," he said as he poured his heart out to the people standing in front of us, though there was a bit of tension in his voice as he spoke. The old man chuckled and rolled his eyes at the end.

"If you and your father truly believed that, why were his captains allowed to harass and purge this town of anyone who wasn't Catholic?" he replied with anger. I started to pay more attention, ignoring my self-drama, and on his words, I looked over to Maximus, who was clearly surprised by this accusation.

"My father nor myself would tolerate that!" he loudly proclaimed, his temper starting to boil over.

"Then why is it that they're no longer here? Forced to live in the forest with nothing but the clothes on their backside? Why was it that he was allowed to rob the people here of all their wealth and those who spoke up were killed instantly? Why was it when we sent a messenger to New Rome to report these issues, not only was he returned without a head, but we all took ten lashes because of it?!" he screeched at us, tears starting to build up. Each accusation, I looked toward Maximus, and each word built his anger up more and more.

"You claimed that you're here for peace and to build a better Europe, but we know the truth! We've suffered through your lies, and we know that Augustus only cares about himself and ruling with absolute power. We are just pawns for his empire, an empire built on the broken backs of the people he crushed, loyal only to himself and his wretched cause! I can speak for all of us that we'd rather die than serve him or YOU!" His voice filled with grief and pain. Despite how little I knew about him, I saw how much Augustus took from this man. Yet here he was, through all the pain, he was still committed to rebelling against Augustus, despite the fact he probably knew he'd fail. He wasn't hiding or pretending to be loyal; he stood true to his words. When I faced the same obstacle, I just accepted my fate like a coward. I rolled over like a dog to them and believed that if I served them well, they would grant me my freedom.

I looked over to Maximus, whose face had been turning redder as the man spoke. He didn't turn to me, he only glared at the old man and spoke to me. "Azul, grab your horse. If these idiots wish to die, then we'll give it to him."

"Maximus, I—" I started to speak but Maximus quickly interrupted with, "Lord Maximus."

"Lord Maximus," I begrudgingly said. "Perhaps we can find another way, we don't need to resort to violence just yet," I quietly tried to reason with him, to try and keep the peace. I placed my hands on his face, trying to make eye contact with him. He looked at me, and I saw how much his anger and hatred warped his face. "You're better than that, Maximus. You said it yourself, you don't want to be that king." I saw his eyes turn to the old man. As I turned around, Raphael rolled his eyes at me.

"Azul, that man has no care for you or me. He'd rather prove to his daddy that he's a killer too and that he's worthy to rule," he cruelly said, staring right at Maximus, no fear, no remorse, just hate.

Maximus chuckled lowly to himself and then whispered, "You dumb bitch."

He immediately shoved me aside and punched Raphael's face, causing the old man to drop. The children started to cry. The men behind us prepped their arrows, but Maximus placed his blade on Raphael's throat, stopping them from firing.

"You dumb old man," he said as he grabbed him by the hair, blood pulsing down his lip and nose. "You and your people were blessed by God to be a part of a great empire and because you cared so much for your *precious* rights and infidels, you chose to disobey *me* and my *father*?" he spat at him. "As far as I'm concerned, when it comes to you peasants, you should've been grateful you were only whipped and not crippled!" He turned his attention to the archers behind him. I sat there, shocked by this sudden change in Maximus. The kind man I spoke to yesterday wasn't there, but, instead, I felt the presence of Louis.

"Listen up, you bastards. This town belongs to me. I will gut this old man like a fish if you do not let us escape. We'll come back with an army. If you're smart, you'll have a white flag up and weapons away; if not, we will kill each and every one of you," he screeched out; the kids started bawling as the mothers tried to help them. I looked around. Everyone was scared, everyone didn't want this to happen but feared what could happen if they didn't act. I thought there was good in Maximus, that with the crown, we could make a better world. But now the blinds on my eyes had come off. I saw the flaws of Maximus, the lies he and Augustus pushed. These people suffered and did all Maximus claimed I should've, and yet their captain was free to do whatever he wanted.

I looked to the old man, and his face brought me back to Adam's face. To that day, he was nearly killed by Louis. Right there, without thought, without planning or mulling over my choices, I launched myself at Maximus. I knocked his blade away, grabbed his arm and broke it, and planted his face into the ground, hard enough to knock him out but not kill him.

The looks on the people's faces were ones of awe and fear. Most of them stood there, frozen by my action. I had assaulted the prince of the New Roman Empire. I had damned these people to a painful and vicious death. As Maximus's face lay in the dirt, the screams of the townspeople riddled my spine. Some of them ran away, locking themselves in their houses, most just stood there. It wasn't until Raphael shook himself back into reality that a sentence was spoken among us.

"What have you done?" he said with fear in his voice.

In the past, I would've taken this time to second-guess myself, asking myself the same thing. Now, though, I knew what I did and why I did it. *Maximus is no saint, neither is his father. They'd burn this town if given the chance.*

"Saving your town," I said to him. I heard his chuckle like I was lying to him.

"Saving us?! How is attacking the prince, the prince whose army is staring us down, the one you *supposedly* swore allegiance to, going to save us from the emperor?!" he screamed at me. I didn't blame him for how he felt. I just rode in with this man, pleaded with them to join our side, and now I chose to do what's right? I saw why he was angry and distrusting, but I had to get them on my side if we were going to win.

"Because we're going to take the fight to them," I valiantly said.

"Tell me, did you just lose your mind and decide to drag all of us down to hell with you!?" he yelled with anger in his voice.

"No, just... listen, okay. Augustus has no idea what's happening here; he has no eyes anymore. We can convince him that your town has surrendered, and when the moment arises, we can take our vengeance on him," I said with a vicious tone, a tone bloodthirsty and looking for revenge.

"How do you suppose to do that? In case you haven't realized, they control a massive army getting ready to charge at us!" he yelled at me.

"But they won't, not when we send his pigeon claiming the town has surrendered. His army is tired, hungry, and probably still drunk or hungover. They are probably finishing their march soon, but if they think there's no need to attack, and if we can convince him to come here tomorrow, their guard will be down, and we can attack tonight. And we don't need to beat them; the only thing we need to do is cut off the head of the serpent. The only reason those men are here is because of Augustus. Once he's dead, they will lose their purpose, their unity, the Empire will collapse, and they will return home," I said to the townsfolk. I could see the terror and confusion on their faces; there was no reason for them to believe this would work. There was no reason they should trust me. Raphael was looking around, no doubt thinking about what to do.

"I know how awful this situation is, how you feel there's no good options available, but I led you down this path without even realizing it. Please let me help you earn your freedom back," I pleaded with them.

The people behind Raphael started to nod their heads in agreement, the fear slowly fading off their faces to something more resolved. Raphael grabbed Maximus's blades from the ground and got on one knee.

"My blade is yours, Azul. We will follow you down this path. We believe in you," he proclaimed to a roar of the crowd.

CHAPTER 17

The tent we were in was small, smaller than most of the tents from Augustus's camp. It seemed like a lifetime ago when I came up with the town's defense against Russell. We had a couple candles lit as it was the dead of night. Most of us tried to be as quiet as possible to make sure there was no chance Augustus would catch wind of our plan.

"Okay, we got about seventy-five people here with pitchforks, butcher knives, some decent swords, and bows and arrows. With how little we have, the last thing we'd want to do is get into an all-out fight with them. What we can do is take advantage of the fact they aren't expecting an attack," I proclaimed to the group of men surrounding me. Each of them was in charge of a battalion who were ready to die for their town, for their freedom.

"We will surround the camp, first killing the patrol guards, then we'll spark fires next to the outer layer of tents, causing the army to be trapped in a wall of fire. You'll continue to launch arrows into the camp, setting the area on fire and killing anyone that tries to escape. While all of this is happening, I'll go inside and kill Augustus," I declared.

It seemed like it didn't take much to convince Augustus we won the town. I set his banner up along with sending a note declaring the town belonged to the New Roman Empire. In it, I *informed* him that the town negotiated a treaty with Maximus and that, due to how long it took, we agreed to make it official tomorrow. He didn't send the pigeon back, but I doubt he was onto us. We had to stay vigilant and keep our guard up, though; one false move, and we were doomed.

Before we left, I needed to do one more thing. I went to the back of the town, through the wall and near the forest. Maximus was tied up on one of the trees, left with his armor but no sword or helmet. His face was scuffed up with cuts and dirt, a bloody nose and a busted lip. He was awake, of course he was, and stared at the dirt. When I walked up, I knew he saw my feet as he turned away, not wanting to give me any attention. The townspeople wanted to kill him, but I talked them out of it. If we were to fail, they could use him as a hostage to try and keep the rest of the people alive.

"Before I go, I need to know something," I said to Maximus coldly. He still refused to meet my eyes. I bent my knees to get right at his level, grabbing his face so he had to look at me. "Were you going to lie to me for my entire life or until I was your wife?" I said with venom in my tongue. He pulled his face out of my clutches and looked away again, but then slowly turned to face me of his own free will.

"I did what I needed to do for this empire, Azul. If telling you what you wanted to hear, that the death of all those you care for wasn't your fault, would've helped bring you into the fold and create a stronger empire, I'd do it again," he said coldly to me.

"Spoken like a truly *pure* man," I repeated to him. "Lying to your people, feeding them false hope and perceptions that aren't true, just like yourself."

He glared at me. "Heavy is the head that wears the crown, Azul. You look at me and think all I am is a liar and fraud. I look at myself as a man willing to do whatever it takes to save civilization. If it means a few white lies here and there, like I said, I'll do it every time," he responded, practically chomping at my face.

"Then if that's the price for civilization, the *powerful* lying to the *weak,* killing and tormenting those who don't agree with them, then civilization shouldn't exist, not without everyone benefiting, not just you!" I screeched at him. His face went back in fear. He was not prepared for my anger to come, and to be honest, neither was I. I took a deep breath and continued. "It doesn't matter anymore. Tonight your empire will collapse."

"You're a bigger fool than I thought if you think you can crush his army with these men. The second you charge at Augustus, you'll die," he mockingly said to me.

"If that's the case, I'll die with my freedom and knowing I did what was right," I announced to the prince. "Goodbye, Maximus. When I come back, I hope you'll see the error of your ways, I hope... you'll be able to be the man you claimed to be," I said as I walked away. I could hear him yelling, trying to get my attention, but I didn't care to listen. His words were just a waste of air to me. I knew who he truly was, and I wouldn't let myself fall down that path again.

As I passed the gate, I felt a headache start to emerge, growing sharper with every second. I could barely think when suddenly the world around me became dark. I felt a grip around my head and then my throat. I felt myself being lifted up, two red eyes emerging from the shadows, staring into my own eyes. I heard nothing except one thing: *Show me your secrets.*

The shadows and pain disappeared as quickly as they came. I felt no pain around my throat or head. I looked around, and there was no one. I was still in the same spot as before, nothing had changed. Perhaps, perhaps my mind was playing tricks on me? Maybe my powers were acting up? No, this felt dark, this felt wrong, like something had invaded my mind. I screamed across the town to hurry and get ready; I didn't know what was going to happen, but I wasn't going to stand around and wait.

We started to line up outside the town to make the march to the camp. By the time we got there, the camp should be dead with only a few guards on patrol. Most of their families were outside, taking one last... *No*, I couldn't think like that. This plan would succeed, it *had* to. Once Augustus was dead, we'd be free. The army would collapse once they realized their emperor was dead, and they'd return home. As I started to walk out, Raphael grabbed my shoulder with a fierce grip.

"Please, Azul, bring these men back home safely," he said with pain in his voice. He wasn't crying, but his eyes were bloodshot, and fear had a tight grip on his face. I placed my hand on his and nodded my head.

"I'll do whatever it takes," I proudly replied. I walked up in front of the crowd, their faces staring at me, looking at their leader to guide them.

"I want to thank all of you for standing by me. You could've easily walked away or sold me out to Augustus, but you stuck with me, and I won't let you down. This is the dawn of a new era, an era of peace and freedom for everyone that strives for it! We will create our own destiny, not forced to be anyone's pawn! Now, let's go!" I screamed to them, to fire them, and myself, up.

I heard their passion for freedom burst through their lungs. They were ready to fight for their lives. We started to take the march right through the forest, all on foot. No words were said during the march, no one wanted to risk being spotted. I played the situation in my head for what seemed like a thousand times on that walk. Most of the men should be asleep with only a few guards. It would take them precious minutes to prepare themselves, but once the fires spread across the camp, they'd be confused and look for a way to escape. It'd provide me with the cover needed to charge Augustus. I had to channel my energy immediately or there was no chance I could get to him given all the men surrounding him. I had one chance. If I didn't kill him immediately, the men would swarm me and capture me again, and my life would end there. One chance at victory, one chance at freedom or death.

After an hour of marching, we finally reached the outskirts of the camp. The place seemed like a ghost town as there was no smoke coming from fires, no singing or laughing from drunken soldiers celebrating their victory, and no guards protecting the camp. Fear started to seep into my head. I knew this was the best time, yet I expected guards and some drunk men out of their tents. Were they prepared? Did they know we were coming? Paranoia started to stick to me like a leech. I refused to believe Augustus had figured us out. There was no way he could've, right? *No*, I thought to myself. *Now cannot be the time for doubt. One misstep, and it would be over for all of us.*

I started to send teams off in different directions to charge the camp, each one carrying unlit torches to keep themselves hidden. We were less of a threat, but with us piercing all sides, they wouldn't be able to mow us down with their superior numbers in one direction. I prepared to light my torch to signal the attack. I stared at the camp to make sure no one was ready for us. I couldn't shake an uneasy feeling in my stomach, but I had to bury it in my mind. There was no way Augustus knew what we were doing. I looked around to the men near me. They nodded their heads as I did. They were ready. I took my torch out and lit it, letting the rest of them know to do it as well and to charge and fight.

The flames lit up the darkness of the forest, but they weren't the only torches. Just as we lit the torches, hundreds more started to light up the camp. It was clear as day: the men were armored up, staring at us, guns and arrows pointed in each direction. We were stopped in our tracks. Not a single man moved. They knew, they knew what we'd do. They knew our plans, they knew how we'd do it, they even knew when we'd show up. My throat started to close in on me. I could barely taste any air coming in, and my head started to squeeze. I couldn't believe my eyes. How the hell could this happen? Augustus's men stood there too, waiting, it seemed, for something. I wasn't sure what exactly; they could mow us down, but they didn't.

Eventually, Augustus emerged from the crowd, as per usual wearing his white armor. He walked right up to me, no weapons in his hand, no torch, no sword by his side, nothing, that is, until he took my torch from me. I couldn't muster the courage to speak; my mind was still racing on how this could even happen. Finally he broke the silence.

"So, was this your plan the entire time, or is this just one of your quickly-hatched schemes?" he said graciously and without emotion. He stared at me with no care about the men surrounding me, no care about anything. He seemingly had all the control in the world. I guess he knew he had nothing to lose. Finally, I found some words to throw out there.

"How?" I feebly replied. My mind was racing, looking for any solution. Maybe there was a spy, maybe he figured out an issue with the pigeon. Something had to tip him off.

"It matters not how I knew, like everything you do, you never think even a second ahead, I don't know what that boy saw in you that made him think you're worth saving," he said. "Did you kill him too, or is he in your pitiful attempt of a raid?" His tone turned hostile, aggressive, and I channeled my own hatred, my own rage, to help rattle the cage within me.

"He's still breathing, he's my captive and mine alone, I refused to be a part of your hypocritical empire, and I decided to finally do what I should've done back that first night I saw you," I said, but he only chuckled.

"I've given you so many opportunities to see what my vision and empire can provide to all in Europe and instead of seeing the positives of it, you only see what you want, the tiny negatives that it comes with," Augustus quietly stated. I tightly gripped my sword below me, my anger beginning to boil.

"Yes, Augustus, the small negative like how you don't care about your people, you only care about making yourself powerful and revolving the world around you and those that come after you. You and your *boy* lied to me from the very start," I screamed at him. My nerves were starting to warm up, my fear turned to hatred.

"And why shouldn't I? If not for me, Europe would still be a pig's sty. I have brought this continent back to where it should be, the crown jewel of civilization, where we'll live a prosperous life."

"On top of the thousands you murdered for not obeying your demands, who'd live peacefully besides your empire, after you killed anyone that had a whiff of rebellion. You're evil, Augustus, pure and simple," I yelled at him. He simply shook his head in disagreement.

"Such a shame that your stupidity poisoned your potential. If you can't see what I'm doing will help turn this continent around, then you must die," he said.

"Why don't you do it yourself then, if you're so high and mighty, you should have no problem killing a woman," I goaded him. I noticed he waved at his men, their guns and bows dropping down immediately. All eyes were on us. He was going to fight me to assert his dominance, at least that's what I was taking from that action. There was no other reason for him to do so when he could have his men fight me instead.

"Go on then, take your blade and end this, end my evil reign right now," he said as he took several steps back and placed his arms out to the side, putting himself in a position of vulnerability.

I felt a smile emerge on my face; the old man blundered it at the end. Yet despite my joy, I still felt this sense of fear and caution. He had complete control of this event and yet he told his men to stand down, offering himself to me. I know what Sadiq told me, but there's no way Augustus could stop me. Even if he, at one point, did have powers, he gave it all to his son. Even if he had any left over, I knew that if I put all of my energy into this blow, it would kill him. I only had one shot at this, I couldn't afford to blunder this either, I had to take advantage of it.

I closed my eyes and focused all the power and speed I had in this one moment. I thought about everything this monster was responsible for. The beatings his captains dished out, victim after victim, the countless bodies he laid on the field, the death of Adam and Charles, my own near death. I could feel the power surge through me; my fear turned to anger, and my anger roared out of me. I took one leap at him, with all my strength coursing through the veins in my arms as I swung my blade right at his head. As I got closer to his face, I saw that he wasn't even looking at me, his eyes were closed. Perhaps he was praying to whatever God he believed in.

I stopped right as we got face-to-face. My blade felt like it was jammed right into his neck, but as I looked up, I saw the sword was in his hand; he'd caught it. I couldn't believe it; how the hell could he do that, how could anyone do that!? I tried to yank the sword out of his hand, but it wouldn't budge, and then I heard a sort of clicking noise coming from Augustus. He opened his blood red eyes, and for the first time, I saw hatred and evil there.

"Even after giving you the opening shot, you continue to disappoint me," he said.

One punch, that was all it took to send me flying into the forest. My ribs felt crushed along with my chest plate. Gunshots started to ring in the air as screams and fighting broke out. As I lay on the ground, I held my stomach and felt the fist mark he left on it. This couldn't be real; how could that old man do this?

"Did you really think you were the only one with gifts? That my name or my *son's* name was the only reason these savages would listen to me, that none of them would challenge me for my empire?" Augustus said right next to me. I jumped away from him, hoping the trees would give me a chance to recover. He moved so fast, he was so strong, if this was real, he had the same powers I did. I tried to keep my distance, but by the time I was on both of my feet, he threw another punch, this time right in my face. I flew across the yard and nearly went twenty feet, crashing through the trees.

"For twenty years, I've had these powers that you know so little about. These gifts are why I will rule Europe, girl, and it will be the reason you die," he said with no emotion in his tone, no mockery in it, just heartless and cold-blooded.

I tried to stand up, but my head was ringing so badly, blood was pouring out of my nose and mouth, my jaw felt cracked and my ribs were like wet bread. It took two seconds for him to reach me and to smack me right into the dirt with one punch to the back of my head.

"You had no chance, Azul. While you rely solely on your instincts and charging up your strikes, I have years of training myself to be the weapon I've become. Your speed, your strength, your powers are nothing compared to mine. My mind is on a level that is incomparable to yours. You should've accepted my *gift* when I offered it, to live in what you claim to be a lie, but you wanted to be a hero," he said in a mocking tone as he stepped on my head, burying it into the dirt. I could barely breathe, but he wasn't trying to smash it, he was toying with me. "It's a shame that it'll take your death for you to realize that heroes don't exist. They never have, and they never will. Men of action and cunning, they're the ones who rule this land." He took his foot off my head, giving me a chance to breathe. As I lay in the dirt, something inside me demanded I reach for his sword. I was defeated, I knew this all too well, but I couldn't give up, my spirit wouldn't let me.

"Even with your broken bones, you refuse to learn your lesson?" he asked me. I could barely focus on his words or the fire and smoke that roared in front of me. The screams and the shots meant nothing to me at that moment. I only focused on the blade and fighting back. He grabbed my right hand with a death grip, the bone cracking under the pressure that came under it. My body was so weak, I couldn't try to break from his grip. All I felt was the cold steel on my wrist and then just pure pain.

He chopped it off. He chopped my hand off. I screamed, weeping like a baby from all the pain I felt across my body. Tears poured down my face; blood gushed from my nose, mouth, and hand. I was broken—a sad, bloody puddle of a girl. A girl in over her head with what she can and can't do.

"This little rebellion is over, but don't worry, girl; I'll make sure you live long enough to see your town destroyed and burnt to the ground, along with each and every one of your friends killed right in front of you. Only then, after your soul and body is completely destroyed, I'll give you the sweet relief of death," he stated effortlessly, tossing my hand right next to my body.

I heard the cackling stomps of a horse coming close to me as I saw Maximus ride up. My body was so weak, I could barely shout or cry. I couldn't move. I just stared at the sky. I realized that I was dead, and I couldn't do anything about it. I closed my eyes and hoped that I would die from blood loss, but one sound, one cry, revitalized my body. I had heard it only a few times, but I knew what it came from. It was the only thing I could hear, the only thing I focused on. The flapping of its wings, the growl growing louder. I tried to crawl away, but my body felt stuck to the ground. Finally, the Dragon landed right in front of us.

The beast stared; its black scales would be practically invisible if it wasn't for the fire behind it. My mind shut everything down around me. I could see that Maximus and Augustus were staring at the Dragon too, but I heard nothing. I knew the fighting was practically over, but I heard nothing from them, all I cared about was the Dragon. It was staring directly at me; its diamond blue eyes watched my every move. I felt the heat starting to build around us. I could see Maximus reaching his hand out. I feared for what was about to happen as the Dragon started to rise up, and I buried my head into my arms and closed my eyes. I felt the heat bake over me. I could see through my closed eyes the fires surrounding me for a few seconds, but it never hit me. When I opened them, I saw ashes in front of me. The trees were broken and scorched. There was a spot where the flames didn't hit, but besides that, the area was incinerated.

I fearfully looked at the Dragon. Steam poured out of its nose. I wasn't sure if I was alive or dead, but I knew I wasn't safe with that beast there. It started to open its mouth, and I feared it was finishing the job as I covered myself up again.

"Run," A deep voice whispered to me. I opened my eyes, looking around to see if there was anyone else talking to me. It was only the beast, moving its head to the side, telling me to escape. I could barely stand, let alone move, but I dragged myself through the forest, away from this nightmare, away from this pain. I ran to the only place I knew; the only place I felt safety in. I ran for home.

The End

www.ingramcontent.com/pod-product-compliance
Lightning Source LLC
Chambersburg PA
CBHW070629310726
48982CB00001B/225

* 9 7 9 8 9 8 8 4 2 7 4 0 7 *